Arcane Arts Anthology

Dear Stepan, 4.5.2017

Congratulations on the full professorship.

Hope you are well,

all the best,

Yui

Herausgeber / Editor

Dr. Kai Herbertz

Herbertz Entertainment UG (haftungsbeschränkt)

Augustastr. 32 / 40477 Düsseldorf / Deutschland

HRB 77850 (Registergericht Düsseldorf)

http://hespiele.de/impressum.htm

1. Auflage 2017

©2017 Dr. Kai Herbertz, Düsseldorf

Alle Rechte vorbehalten / all rights reserved

Autoren / Authors:

The Dark Siren ©2015 by Danielle E. Shipley and Tirzah Duncan

Escape! ©2016 by Michelle Proulx

Prophet Motive ©2016 by Edd Vick

Petri Parousia ©2005 by Matthew Hughes

A Midsummer Night ©2016 by Elisa Bonnin

The Twelfth Witch ©2016 by Juliana Rew

Robyn's Gift ©2016 by A. M. Kremer

Arcane Arts ©2016 by Katharina Gerlach

Tartarus Bound ©2016 by Kai Herbertz

No Time to Lose ©2016 by Ariana Tiens

Ars Aeterna ©2016 by A. H. Archer

Umschlagillustration / Cover Design: Lieu Pham of Covertopia.com
Lektorat / Copy Edit: Red Adept Publishing, Michelle Proulx
Druck: Createspace, a DBA of On-Demand Publishing LLC
CreateSpace Independent Publishing Platform
Printed in the U.S.A.
Artikelnummer: 2017010001
ISBN-13: 978-1543071559
ISBN-10: 1543071554

Das Werk, einschließlich seiner Teile, ist urheberrechtlich geschützt. Jede Verwertung ist ohne Zustimmung des Verlages unzulässig. Dies gilt insbesondere für die elektronische oder sonstige Vervielfältigung, Übersetzung, Verbreitung und öffentliche Zugänglichmachung.
All characters and events in this book are fictitious and any resemblance to real persons, living or dead, is purely coincidental.

Dedication

To Ravindra "Ravi" Ramrattan (2. Sep.1983 – 21. Sep. 2013).

Acknowledgements

This collection of short stories would not exist if it were not for the support of friends, family, and Kickstarter supporters. I am grateful for the tremendous support of the "Knight" level Kickstarter backers: Tatia (ALE) :), Stefan Gunnar Sveinsson, Henry Bentley, Wing-Onn Chan, Steve Deng, Declan Waters, Nathan Duby, Anil A, Don, Beth & Meghan Ferris, Mike Scott Thomson, Florian Dietrich, Philip Bonhard, Martha Benco, Fay K., and Nina K.

In addition, there were three Technomage supporters and even though a specific shoutout was not part of the reward tier, I still want to mention them here: Jannis S., Marc E., and Nils H. thank you for the support!

My brother Armin came through as the Hero of the Realm – truly, you have made this anthology possible!

I am grateful for the many awesome authors that contributed to the anthology: Danielle E. Shipley and Tirzah Duncan, Michelle Proulx, Edd Vick, Matthew Hughes, Elisa Bonnin, Juliana Rew, A. M. Kremer, Katharina Gerlach, Ariana Tiens, and A. H. Archer.

Speaking of authors, fellow author and host (along with Veronica Belmont) of Sword & Laser, Tom Merritt, kindly agreed to write a powerful foreword for the anthology. Thank you so much for the support!

Editing suggestions were provided by Red Adept Editing and also by freelance editor Michelle Proulx.

Finally, I am grateful for the cover design by Lieu Pham of Covertopia.com.

Kai Herbertz January 2017

Foreword

Thank you for picking up this anthology. Pour yourself a cup of coffee and sit down. I know you're going to enjoy this. Because I've done an anthology before. There's something in the process of making an anthology that results in stories that give a jolt to your imagination the way that a cup of joe does to the rest of your mind.

Anthologies are hard. As a publisher you're trying to convince readers to take a chance not on one story but on several. And if you're making a good anthology, you can't easily explain them all. That's why anthologies often have a theme. At least you can promise people stories about alien artifacts, or death machines or swords and laser. Or in our case here, arcane arts.

As a writer anthologies are difficult too. You need to create a compelling story in a short amount of space. You want to deliver on the promise of the wider anthology but stand out on your own at the same time. If you're really good, the reader remembers your stories out of the many others.

Anthologies aren't easy for editors either. You must go through literally hundreds to thousands as many stories as you'll put in the book. Now, I see some of you snickering, imagining all the bad stories one needs to wade through to find the gems. And yes, there are always duds. But those are easy. It's the good stories that make it hard.

There are always more good stories than you can fit in your anthology. Always people you have to disappoint even though they don't deserve it. Maybe you have two equally great stories about the Titans. Maybe there are three excellent tales of Filipino immigrants. Maybe a half dozen stories start with a skeleton and they're all great. And you have to choose.

But that's why anthologies are worth reading. It's not because they're the cream of the crop. It's because they're an interesting collection of excellence. An anthology is a balanced organically grown hand selected artisan's brew of stories. An anthology can deliver a wider breadth of flavors and exciting beats than a single story. An anthology is a series of shots of espresso compared to the novel's tall latte.

So line up your cups folks. Our story baristas are about to pour a range of stories from the mellow and satisfying re-imagination of greek mythology, to the spiky dark roast of escape rooms to the rich and smooth appeal of a congregation of philosophical aliens interpreting your every move.

Enjoy responsibly.

Tom Merritt   November 2016

Table of Contents

Dedication..6
Acknowledgements...7
Foreword..9
Table of Contents...12
Ars Aeterna by A. H. Archer...................................13
The Dark Siren by Danielle E. Shipley and Tirzah Duncan..36
Petri Parousia by Matthew Hughes.........................69
No Time to Lose by Ariana Tiens 85
A Midsummer Night by Elisa Bonnin....................122
Arcane Arts by Katharina Gerlach 142
Prophet Motive by Edd Vick..................................173
Robyn's Gift by A. M. Kremer 197
Escape! by Michelle Proulx...................................216
The Twelfth Witch by Juliana Rew........................248
Tartarus Bound by Kai Herbertz...........................276
About the Authors..299

Ars Aeterna
by A. H. Archer
Translated by Kai Herbertz

"What do we have?" Magistrate Al'Beike, the director of the Grand Art Academy of Faustberg, strode through the ranks of arcane artists. Now and then he stopped, took notes, and occasionally handed out praise and accolades.

"Er, hmmm, what … is that?" the bewildered magistrate asked while contemplating the painting of a young non-human artist.

The paint-blotted female lizardman hissed with embarrassment. The image showed a building made of red bricks, which were used nowhere in these climes. Large black characters were displayed on the building, spelling ARS AETERNA. Characters that did not belong to any known language. In any case, neither the customary hieroglyphs of Ka'Zan nor the runic script that was used in Faustberg contained similar symbols. The characters of merchants from faraway lands were also different.

Even though this greatly displeased the magistrate, the curved, metallic, gleaming carriages which were placed in front of the building angered him the most. Compared to the obviously passing-by pedestrians, who wore depressingly inelegant clothes, these carriages were far too low to be practical, and they stood in such close proximity that harnessing of horses seemed to be impossible.

"How long did you work on that?" the magistrate asked grumpily.

The lizard answered brokenly in the common tongue. "Two weeks."

The magistrate took the painting off the easel. "Too slow and too horrendous!" he said angrily. He ripped up the painting and threw the shreds at the face of the motionless lizardman. "You are supposed to paint Ka'Zan. Why doesn't that get through your thick skull?" Enraged, he walked on.

"Cleaning duty for Glark!" he shouted. "For one week!" he added.

Glark'Gamnan, the female lizardman, lowered her head despondently. Not only did she have to start from the beginning, but she also had to tidy up after her not particularly cleanliness-minded artist colleagues. Hopefully she would get a better vision that satisfied the magistrate. She closed her eyes and entered a trance.

Three meters away, a bearded dwarf was occupied with building a diorama. The magistrate had specifically praised him. Gmin was happy. He did not want to be treated like Glark'Gamnan. He had learned his lesson and took particular care with the details of the model. The palace of Ka'Zan was mostly completed. One could remove the roof and examine the winding corridors inside. The architects had apparently created a kind of maze, which Gmin minutely reconstructed and modelled with wood and plaster.

Bolb walked up to him. The orc grunted something, which Gmin ignored.

"Try hard!" Bolb said eventually in his begrudging manner.

"That rather applies to you!" Gmin mumbled into his beard. The dwarf nodded toward Bolb's workspace.

A life-sized marble statue of a finely clothed elf stood there. The statue was colorfully painted in the current fashion. It almost seemed to be alive.

"Who is that supposed to be?" Gmin asked.

"No idea," Bolb grunted. "The magistrate wanted me to model some elven dandy from Ka'Zan. I think he's the governor. I had to concentrate very hard to see him. Gave me a splitting headache, I'm telling you."

The dwarf frowned. "That's a surprise. I didn't think you could get headaches," he taunted, and shifted his attention back to his diorama.

By nightfall, only a few artists worked in the atelier. Everyone was free to decide when to work on their art, so long as they delivered useful results. After all, creativity could not be planned.

Glark'Gamnan was also still present. She had to be, because now it was time to clean the atelier. For two or three hours she was busy with scrubbing the floor, taking the trash to the river, and procuring fresh materials for the artists.

Everyone had received a more or less specific task from the magistrate. Glark'Gamnan had initially assumed that all tasks were completely different, but now that she had ample opportunity, more than she had wished for, to study the works of the other artists, she noticed that there were several duplicates.

Especially when it came to the palace of Ka'Zan—it was noticeably often depicted in paintings, sketches, and models. Presumably presents were being created for an imminent visit of state.

The magistrate had asked her to focus on the city of Ka'Zan as a whole and then to let her gaze wander. However, she was just not succeeding. Her thoughts always took her to another place, and she and the others did not know what to make of it. Where did these images come from? Did that place even exist, or was it pure imagination? Was she no arcane artist in the end, but simply untalented?

Sorrowful, she moved to her austere bedchamber. Tomorrow, a new long day waited for her.

Ars Aeterna

***

"The prince will see you now!"

The attendant bowed to the emissary of Ka'Zan, who was introduced as Lord Eólon. The elf and his bodyguards spared a bored glance for the servant of Prince Radebrecht of Faustberg. Dressed in light, flowing garments, the delegation strode through the endless corridors of the prince's residence until they came to the entrance of the audience chamber. Two servants opened the enormous double doors.

***

"Welcome, honoured guests!" With a fake friendliness the prince greeted the guests who had travelled from the remote city.

Ka'Zan and Faustberg were the two metropolises in the icy wastes of Coralt. While Faustberg was situated at the northern edge of the ice and bordered milder regions, Ka'Zan lay at the foot of the endless mountains.

Icy cold surrounded Ka'Zan, but through unknown means (in Faustberg people speculated it was due to a volcano) it continuously remained warm in Ka'Zan. Pleasantly warm. Ka'Zan drew its wealth from the endless mountains. The mithril prospectors lived a hard and deprived life, and when they had mined enough of the silvery metal they came to Ka'Zan to trade it for wares, food, and different services. In addition, Ka'Zan was the final destination of the merchant caravans from the southeast, from beyond the icy wastes.

Prince Radebrecht had always looked at what he considered an inappropriate profit of Ka'Zan with envy and greed. Gladly he would have claimed a part, preferably the bulk of it, for himself.

The prince had spread various sketches of the atelier by the arcane artists on his massive desk. The ink-drawn scrolls were arranged in such a way that they could not be seen by the delegation from Ka'Zan.

"Prince Radebrecht," a black-clad advisor, who inconspicuously stood in a corner of the room, said. "What about the present for our guests?"

The prince shook his head barely noticeably, went through a drawer, and retrieved a bottle of expensive liquor.

The negotiations dragged on for a while but ultimately finished without results. The delegation from Ka'Zan received an expensive but not unusual present, a flask of Tolarian ether liquor, and was finally bade farewell to return to Ka'Zan.

When the prince was alone with his advisor, the latter asked for an explanation. "My prince, was the plan changed?"

Ars Aeterna

Prince Radebrecht replied in a whisper. "That wasn't Lord Eólon, steward of Ka'Zan."

He slid the latest sketch of the arcane artists over to the black-clad man. The man narrowed his eyes and then nodded slowly. "Yes, however very similar." Then he added, "Remarkable how much effort was apparently spent in Ka'Zan to find a doppelgänger of someone who virtually never appears in public. You'd think that a remote lookalike would be sufficient."

The prince drummed with his fingers on the desktop. He always did so whenever he was in deep thought.

"Well, their success justifies the effort, I'd say. In that case we have to implement an alternative plan. What was the man's name again? Snark? Could you hire him?"

***

The agent entered the Grand Art Academy of Faustberg. His non-glossy black uniform identified him as a high-ranking government official. The man walked up to the magistrate and quietly spoke a few words. The magistrate nodded mutely. Then the agent straightened, nodded curtly to the magistrate, and left the building.

Pensive, magistrate Al'Beike withdrew into his study chamber.

A. H. Archer

The next morning the magistrate made his usual circuit through the atelier of the arcane artists. A handful of employees of the academy followed him. Now and then he stopped and decided, often under the protest of the affected artist, that the work was finished and the art would be sold.

Usually works of art were put up at the next vernissage after the artist declared them to be finished. The prince's agents were the first to buy them at a fixed rate. Afterward the remaining pieces of art would go on public auction together with the creations of other branches of the art academy.

Things were different this time. The employees of the academy packed up statues, paintings, models, and other works of art and took them away, while other employees took their places. The diorama of the palace of Ka'Zan, which Gmin worked on, disappeared just like the statue of Eólon, on which Bolb applied the finishing touch. The only remaining works of art were those that were obviously in the early stages, as well as the paintings created by a redheaded elf who worked in the farthest corner of the atelier and who was ignored by the magistrate, and Glark'Gamnan's latest painting.

There was not much to see in the painting, yet. A wide river separated the canvas into two halves. On the upper side the silhouette of a city emerged.

Ars Aeterna

The magistrate grumbled malcontentedly. "I'm not aware that a river flows through Ka'Zan," he said irately.

"I paint what I see," Glark'Gamnan replied evenly. Her eyes were twisted. She was in a trance.

Unhappy, the magistrate walked on. His face twisted when he inspected the paintings of the redheaded elf. The elf always painted fire. This time a snakelike shape occupied the center of the fire. *That's supposed to be a dragon,* the magistrate thought.

The elf weirded him out, which was why he did not chastise him. He would love nothing better than to throw him out of the art academy. His paintings were useless. They showed nothing of relevance—the underworld perhaps, who should know? In any case, none of his paintings were ever bought by the prince's agents, and they only yielded meager profits at the auctions. But the elf possessed the aura of a madman. One had to be careful around such people.

The magistrate would simply unleash his anger on the female lizardman. Perhaps that would teach the elf a lesson not to produce further worthless art. *But not right now, later!* The magistrate moved to one of the large windows. Outside, soldiers marched past on the broad main street right in front of the academy. The guard left the city, toward the icy wastes. *They are probably on their way to an exercise, just as they often are during summer,* the magistrate thought.

A. H. Archer

***

Without a sound, the grapple became entangled in the wooden wall of the palace. A permanent silencing spell protected the assassin's gear. Snark was one of the best of his profession and certainly the best who was currently available in Faustberg. Money was not an issue for Prince Radebrecht, and so even the advance was more than a good craftsman earned in a year. Snark smiled while he climbed the wall with his rope. The plans he had received beforehand for the residence of Ka'Zan, which he now broke into, had been extremely detailed. This assignment would be child's play.

Snark reached a window which was—his heightened senses alerted him to it—magically secured. He reached into a bag on his belt and retrieved a vial with a blue liquid, which he immediately spread in a fine layer over the window frame with a vaporizer. Afterward the window was easy to pry open, which he accomplished without a sound, and—thanks to the vapor he had applied before—without raising an alarm.

The corridor beyond the window was dark. Snark had inherited night vision from his orcish mother and dexterity from his father, who had been a goblin. Silently he glided through the corridor, perfectly succeeding in orienting himself in the darkness. He had studied the plans of the residence in depth and memorized them.

Finally he reached his destination undetected. He slid the paper wall to the side and entered the sleeping quarters of the steward. The characteristic spicy smell of tatami mats filled his sensitive nose.

Without a sound he drew his sword and pierced the prone, seemingly sleeping, figure.

A sizzling sound alerted him, and he leaped back in time to avoid being gravely hit by the explosive trap. The body had been a decoy, prepared with an explosive alchemist's spell. Stunned, Snark shook his head as the burning paper walls were moved to the side and the steward's armored guards stormed into the room.

An ordinary human would have been helpless, but Snark was neither human nor ordinary. He bit down on a hollow tooth in the upper left part of his jaw. The tooth snapped and released a drug. It took all of his strength and endurance to parry the attackers' blows, and he had to back away step by step. However, with every step a bit of his fatigue fell away and the attackers slowed down. At least, so it seemed to him.

For the guards of the steward, the situation unfolded differently. The stocky masked shape of the assassin could barely parry the practiced coordinated sword thrusts. The intruder was good but lost more and more ground, backing away toward the wall. The end was predictable.

But suddenly his eyes turned blood red. His movements sped up and became more precise. He did not back away anymore, launching a counterattack instead. The swords clanked a few more times before the guards collapsed one by one, fatally hit or severely wounded from the whirling slashes of the assassin.

Panting, Snark left the sleeping quarters. The drug would take its toll. A season of his life expectancy was used up in an instant. Still, if he had not used the drug, he would not have reached the natural end of his life, of that he was sure. In his line of work capture meant torture, followed by even more torture, and finally execution.

To ultimately avoid that nasty fate, he had implanted another hollow tooth on the right side of his jaw that was filled with poison. He hoped that he would not need it today.

There was a commotion in the lodging. Snark had already booked the mission as a failure. He would blame his incomplete information. This was no way to work! The steward should have been in his sleeping quarters, as they had assured him.

Yet things had developed differently. Snark's escape route led him past a window. Snark glanced incidentally through the window into the inner courtyard. Eólon, the steward of Ka'Zan, fled toward the stables, where a coach waited. Several guards surrounded him for protection. Snark inhaled deeply and took the bow from his shoulder. He nocked an arrow, drew the string, and exhaled. Then he held his breath and took aim. The angle and offset had to be exact. Dexterity, years of practice, and the extraordinary quality of his weapon came together.

The arrow flew in a parabola and pierced the elf's unprotected shoulder seconds later. Snark turned away to leave the building. He knew that the venom of the desert scorpion he had prepared the arrowhead with would do the rest. Even in the thousand-miles-distant Al'Khabib, where the venom originated, no reliable antidote existed. Here in Ka'Zan the venom and its symptoms were largely unknown. *All is well that ends well,* Snark thought. He squeezed through a different window and began to glide down the steep wall of the building.

His elven boots held him upright during his run and enabled him to get down without falling. Nevertheless, he slipped close to the ground, losing contact with the wall and landing abruptly on the pavement. The earth trembled and shook. A deep grumble could be heard. Snark pulled himself together. He had broken several bones due to the fall, and every move hurt, but he forced himself to continue.

A. H. Archer

A mighty roar of thunder cracked behind him. He did not want to turn around, but the red glow that illuminated the street in front of him all of a sudden made him curious. What he saw terrified him, and terror was something the half-orc had banished from his emotions ever since his childhood.

The palace of Ka'Zan stood ablaze, or rather what was left of the palace. A lava fountain burst from its center. Burning debris hurled through the sky and crashed down again. The half-orc turned away and started to run. Panic caught hold of him and made him overcome pain, injury, and fatigue. The fire spread to the city, and the inhabitants of Ka'Zan streamed onto the streets. Fire, everywhere was fire.

***

Marshal Zampo dined in his tent. It was bitterly cold outside. The army of Faustberg camped in the wilderness somewhere between Faustberg and Ka'Zan. His troops did not know the orders, which he had buried deep inside, at the very bottom, of his coat pocket.

They still thought it to be a maneuver that hopefully would not last too long. He had to make them sustain their beliefs for a while longer.

Suddenly the tent flap was lifted and a stocky person entered the tent. The half-orc was badly wounded, his face disfigured by extensive fresh burns, which apparently were only superficially treated. Snark approached the marshal, who backed away with a start.

"Mission accomplished," the half-orc croaked.

As promised, the marshal handed over a small leather pouch. Snark checked its contents and then said: "I'm gone!"

He vanished as quickly and abruptly as he had appeared.

As soon as the assassin was gone, the marshal stepped outside of his tent for the early-morning roll call.

An officer called out "Soldiers," followed by a stretched out "Attention!"

The troops stood still as the marshal gave the order to break camp and be on the march as soon as possible.

***

Magistrate Al'Beike was in a bad mood. The academy's financial situation did not look bright. Even though the income was high, the expenses had constantly risen over the years. They had pompously offered room and board to every mediocre artist, and catering at the academy was not bad, and thus costly. In particular, the branch of the arcane artists used up exquisite and expensive materials. The latest royal commission had drained many unfinished pieces of art from the market. The prince's agents then used the unfinished state as a justification for paying a reduced price. The magistrate was unable to put a stop to this practice.

He would have to downsize his academy to ensure its survival. For far too long they had depended on the prince's benevolence, had heeded the prince's bizarre requests for the paintings, and had the arcane artists operate in that direction. And now this! The magistrate was livid. They had told him that the prince's demand would be greatly reduced.

The goal was reached, the agent had informed him. Whatever that meant.

Al'Beike found out to his relief that the crazy red-haired elf had apparently disappeared on his own accord. A single one of his nonsensical fire paintings remained behind, but otherwise the work space was tidy and deserted.

The magistrate stepped up to Glark'Gamnan's easel. "I've told you a hundred times!" he barked at the lizardman. "This is useless! You stupid lizard!" The magistrate slapped Glark's bald head with the palm of his hand. The slap had the desired effect.

For Glark'Gamnan, the humiliation stung worse than the not insignificant pain. She ducked and endured more abuse.

Rage filled the magistrate as he drove the lizard out of the atelier. He chased her down the stairs for a few steps before he turned back to the other artists, who stared at him, horrified.

Ars Aeterna

He shouted, "From now on things will be different around here!"

He already felt better. He fired three more artists and was about to discard their works before he thought better of it. They would sell for some amount of money, and the academy could use every penny.

***

Sorrowful, Glark'Gamnan looked back at the academy. What was she thinking? She was no arcane artist. None of her paintings had meant anything. They were all weird scenarios, as if they belonged to another world, without any connection to reality. Her time as an arcane artist was over, and she decided to start over somewhere else with a new profession. As a lizardman she could last for a long time without food, and so she left the city to never return to Faustberg.

***

Shortly before dawn, in the coldest hours of the night, Marshal Zampo, who had been appointed by Prince Radebrecht to lead the battle, and his guards assembled on the hill that overlooked the plains of Ka'Zan. Arcanists accompanied them and mounted a scrying sphere that allowed Prince Radebrecht to witness the impending battle from the safety of his fireplace room in his castle in Faustberg.

A. H. Archer

Fire could be seen in the distance of this otherwise black night. The city of Ka'Zan apparently stood in flames. *There must have been riots after the death of the steward,* the marshal speculated. The conquest of the city would be easy pickings, as planned.

The troops of Faustberg took formation. While the flanks were formed by improvised peasant groups, Marshal Zampo ordered the prince's city guard to position themselves at the foot of the hill. He placed behind them the archers, who were supposed to switch position with the guards as soon as the enemy moved out in order to whittle them down with volleys of arrows. If the opposing troops got too close, the guards and the archers would switch back positions.

The marshal still had his trump card up his sleeve. In sight of the hill, hidden in a trench, a hundred armored riders—the pride of the prince's troops—waited for the order to attack. They would strike quickly, break the enemy lines, cause panic, and then mercilessly hunt down the fleeing routed enemy formations. That was the plan.

The sun slowly rose above the mountains east of the city. Trumpets and horns were blown. The army began to march. Not even a quarter hour later the enemy approached, but to the soldiers' horror it was not Ka'Zan's militia.

Ars Aeterna

With a deafening sound a screeching dragon flew past the army of Faustberg. While the less-disciplined sections broke away in panic, Zampo retained a relatively level head and quickly issued improvised orders. In order to avoid a full-blown panic, it was important to remain in control. The soldiers had to notice that he had a plan and was able to handle the situation, even though that was not really the case. Skirmishes with dragons or other flying monsters were rare in this day and age. Probably they had always been rare.

There were old texts that told of such occurrences, but Zampo did not know anyone who had truly met a dragon. Certainly, every once in a while someone claimed to have seen a dragon in the sky. However, the witnesses were usually of ill repute. In any case, this was a real dragon.

Zampo acted. He let the troops take loose formations with wide distances between the individual soldiers. The necessary additional space was freed up by the rout of the peasant militia. Spears at the ready, the troops cowered on the ground. The only way to defeat a dragon in a battle was to ground it as soon as possible. For that reason Zampo had issued the order to sever the dragon's leathery wings.

The dragon, however, had no intention of behaving according to military doctrine. In passing, he turned a few soldiers into living torches with his fire breath. The stumbling, screaming victims reduced the already-low morale to absolute zero. When the dragon began to tear into the left flank with claws, teeth, and tail lashes, the regular troops were routed as well. The dragon bellowed and gleefully devoured some victims, but only for a short time in order to continue spreading fear and terror.

Around noon, the battle was over. The panicked retreat had surely cost as many casualties as the dragon's initial attacks, but it did not end there. The dragon chased after the fleeing soldiers. Only those troops that split up and did not head home would eventually survive. The magical scrying sphere with which Prince Radebrecht had planned to observe his triumph lay buried in the muddy soil.

***

While the dragon was on the way to Faustberg, Prince Radebrecht had already recognized the danger and removed himself from the city. The greedy man pays twice, according to an old folk wisdom, which rang true once more. He thought he had made a surefire bet, but he had nevertheless lost everything. Faustberg used to be a successful and powerful city-state. Perhaps that was the problem. If one does not have anything to do, one looks for a pastime.

He had been set on expansion and had gambled away everything. Pondering, the prince sat inside of his coach, which should take him to Port Trabun. From there he would ferry to Ifflholm, where he hoped to find refuge with his

Ars Aeterna

cousin. At least until it was safe to return. Who would have imagined that the legends were true in the end? Ka'Zan had been built on top of a dragon's cave, after all. According to legend, the stewards of Ka'Zan kept the dragon, who provided warmth, in hibernation with a soul pact. An oasis within the icy wastes, heated by a small dose of dragon's breath.

The arcane artists should have seen that! The guidelines this incompetent magistrate had given them must have been too strict, the prince thought. He should have made the effort to visit the arcane artists from time to time, but now it was too late for that.

***

Faustberg stood in flames. Without any of the troops that should have defended the city, it was at the mercy of the dragon. The dragon had slighted the castle. Disappointed that the prince had not been there, he had proceeded to set houses in several districts on fire with his breath before starting back.

The city's firefighters were overwhelmed. The fires spread ever farther, and Faustberg threatened to share the same fate as Ka'Zan. In some parts the flames spread faster, in other parts slower.

Only a few fires burned at the art academy, but there were still too many to be put out. The artists trickled out into the open. The flames licked at the easels of the gallery in which the art for sale was put up.

***

"Perhaps Magistrate Al'Beike did wrong by her," said Gmin, who stopped briefly on his way out. Bolb grunted in response, but then joined Gmin to contemplate the painting he inspected. A frown on his face, creasing his forehead, he sceptically eyed the piece of art.

"Perhaps Glark'Gamnan was able to see a place after all …" Gmin said. He pointed at the painting in front of them. In the foreground, smiling people could be seen at a fun fair or something of that sort.

"Perhaps the place she saw was not in this world," Gmin continued. Bolb squinted and looked at the details. The picture was, like most of Glark'Gamnan's works, foreshortened. In the middle was a wide river. An unusual bridge construction with high pillars and supporting ropes crossed it.

"Perhaps this place that Glark painted all the time was paradise," Gmin concluded.

The orc's eyes brightened. "Paradise?"

Bolb then slowly nodded in approval. He looked at the colossal buildings on the other side of the river. A tower that rose like a needle into the sky with the top extended like a spindle. A glass-like building that looked like a rectangular gate of enormous size, but free standing and not as part of a city wall as one would expect. The river was filled with large, long-stretched boats, but Glark had drawn neither men nor horses, nor ropes for towing, nor sails. The long, flat black ships moved as if by magic both up- and downstream. Many houses could be seen. Tens of thousands—no, hundreds of thousands of humans, dwarves, or elves had to live there.

"Yes, that's paradise!" Bolb whispered appreciatively.

The Dark Siren
by Danielle E. Shipley and Tirzah Duncan

"You're a skeleton."

I look down from my contemplation of the metallic kidney bean that calls itself "The Cloud Gate" to the figure materialized at my side. By the sound alone, I'd have guessed it was music—something with a flute, maybe piped through a speaker I hadn't known to be situated near my shoes. Instead, it's a small boy, his age not far into the double digits, if he's reached them at all. Round cheeks, mussed black hair, wide eyes blinking at me. I don't blink back, having no eyelids—or eyes, for that matter.

"Yes, I am," I acknowledge.

No point in denying the obvious. I do what I can to downplay some of the visual shock by covering up in long coats with high collars, hats with the brims pulled low, gloves, etc. But the fact is, a fleshless woman is going to attract attention, even in a big city like Chicago where the locals are more or less accepting of the concept. Maybe the kid's a tourist. If his small-town parents run up in a prejudiced panic, things could get difficult fast. Of course, there'd only be myself to blame. I know better than to kill time around a tourist trap like Millennium Park in summer.

"Why are you a skeleton?" the boy's little flute-voice asks next.

Again, I go with the obvious truth. "Necromancy."

I'm hoping that either the kid will move on or the wind will shift. The cigar clamped between my naked teeth is putting out more smoke than is strictly healthy for a body with lungs.

The boy's lips purse in an offended pout. "I know that. Anyone would know that. But how does it work, being a talking, smoking skeleton?" His brow furrows dubiously. "You're not a thrall, are you?"

Thralls—dead or undead servants bound to the magic that made them.

I take a long puff. Hold the smoke in 'til it starts to leak out my eye sockets. Release the rest through my mouth to the overcast sky. "Nope, not a thrall," I assure him. Not for a long time.

"I thought not. You seem too sentient, and you don't move like them. You move like you're alive."

"I am."

"*Reeeeeally?*" He lights up like he's walked into his own surprise party. "A *living* skeleton? That's amazing! How did you do it?"

Danielle E. Shipley and Tirzah Duncan

This isn't shaping into the kind of discussion I need to have with somebody's child. I look around, searching among the thin sea of amblers. "Where are your parents, kid?"

His cherubic face takes on an expression tragic enough to knife through heartstrings. "I don't have parents."

"All right." I carry on through my sudden urge to choke up, never mind that I couldn't produce tears if I wanted to. "Who looks after you, then?"

"Nobody." Abruptly, he giggles. "Hehe, get it?" The next instant, every inch of him below the neck fades into thin air. "No body!"

I'd let my jawbone fall slack, but this cigar's not even half burned down. Waste not—especially when you can burn through a full box on a light week.

"So," I say, when the kid's still-grinning head is rejoined with the rest of him. "You're a ghost."

"No," he says cheerfully. "Just a soul. I do have a body, though." His face falls. "He's not very nice to me. He thinks he's too busy for it. And important. And *old*." His eyes brighten. "I'm going to ask him how to make a living skeleton!"

Another drag of smoke. "Because he's old?"

"Because he's the Dark Siren."

I stare at him. "The who?"

The Dark Siren

"The Dark Siren," he repeats, adding in a low, eerily melodic tone, *"He who sings to the dead."*

"A necromancer," I say flatly. It figures. Where there's a bodiless soul running around, somewhere there's a soulless body. And the only people I've ever encountered who willingly removed their souls were necromancers. Powerful ones.

Creature of necromancy though I am, I can't say the notion fills my rib cage with joy.

"Well, you can give him my regards," I say, tipping my hat and walking away, in case the kid missed that as a dismissal.

"No, I can't," he says, trotting up to keep pace alongside me. "I can't give your regards without knowing your name."

"I sent them without knowing yours," I point out.

"Sure you know it. You've said it." He pitches his voice into a mimicry of mine. "'*Where are your parents, Kid?*'"

A kid named Kid. Lack of parental involvement, confirmed.

My generally curt replies and long stride do nothing to deter the little soul. He follows me all over the park and through the city, appearing to vanish during the train ride back to my neighborhood, but still undeniably present; his singsong chatter never leaves my side. His body back home apparently not much for company, it seems Kid spends his days roaming the earth in search of entertainment—up to and including semi-sociable skeletons. I don't work up the heart to tell him to scram until I reach my bungalow on the South Side.

"It's been nice talking to you," I say, not one-hundred percent dishonestly, "but I've got a lot of work to do, so … I should get to it."

"Oh. All right," he says, his disappointment evident. "Good-bye, Living Skeleton. You've been nice."

One tries.

Inside, I hang up my hat and trench coat. I leave the gloves on, as they improve dexterity, and I leave the other clothes on, because who takes off all their clothes as soon as they walk in the door? Just because I don't have any skin and flesh underneath doesn't mean I wouldn't feel naked without them.

"Weird kid," I say aloud to the room, shaking my skull. I'm not wholly sure how I feel about him. On the one hand, he's a fellow victim of a necromancer. On the other hand, isn't he sort of a necromancer himself? "Nah," I decide. "He's just a kid."

Heading into my office, I settle into the leather chair and open my humidor. Inhaling deeply—not being a necromancer myself, I couldn't begin to explain what keeps me breathing and speaking, but I expect it's right up there

The Dark Siren

with what keeps me thinking and moving—it seems as though I can almost smell the cigars' fine tobacco. Selecting one, I set it between my teeth and light it up.

Some of my senses were burned away with my body. What remains to me is: sight, apparently functioning just as it did when I had eyeballs and nerves; sound, just as if I had eardrums; and a dim sensation of touch. Taste vanished along with my tongue and my need for food, but I'm sometimes sure I can perceive the ghosts of scent.

Probably it's psychosomatic, but what should I care? If I can enjoy my cigars, and I have no lungs to ruin, I'm going to keep enjoying them. Whether by use of an olfactory sense nowhere in evidence or by the trick of a brain-free psyche, I'm no worse off.

But now, it's time for work. I pick up a sheaf of papers, scan for where I left off, and pick up my phone. Punching in the number, I brace myself to be screamed at.

"Good evening. Is Mrs. Phillison available? Lovely, thank you. This is Lynn, calling on behalf of Thin-and-Now Food Metrics. I understand you expressed an interest in hearing more about—"

My skull jerks away from the phone. Just because I don't have eardrums doesn't mean I can't feel as if they're rupturing. Even so, I'm used to it by now. It's not as if I haven't been getting screamed at for more than three centuries. At least with telemarketing, it's not personal.

"I'm very sorry. I'd understood that you indicated interest in being contacted after reading an article on the Thin-and-Now website. Is there anyone in your household who might have used your—yes—certainly, I'm very sorry. I'll take your name off the list. Good evening."

I hang up, take another puff on my cigar, and continue to forge my way through the list, looking for people who checked the box deliberately, or anyone polite enough to hear me out anyway.

It's a good field for me, telemarketing. I have the selfsame voice I burned with, the pleasant voice of a woman in her late teens. I can make it sound perkier or more mature as it pleases me, and it has none of a smoker's croak or rattle. I didn't pick up the habit until a century or so after my execution.

My execution. That was during the Würzburg Necromancer Trials, ironically. A big necro-scare swept southern Germany in the late fifteen- and early sixteen-hundreds, and loads of us were burned at the stake. As far as I know, I was the only one to survive the incident, thanks to the vindictive so-called mercies of an actual necromancer.

"*Guten Abend*, Babelin," I remember him calling as I walked along the bridge, mere months before my life came

The Dark Siren

to an end of sorts. He accosted me with a glass of wine in either hand. "But the night is not nearly as lovely as you are. A drink to your health—come, don't be rude."

I took the compliments with a smile, but if I'd taken every glass of wine proffered to me on that bridge, I'd never have known a sober moment. "You flatter me, Lorenz," I told the young man, and swanned on my way, to smile at more compliments and decline more offers. He was insistent, though, and went beyond acceptable flattery. He incited me to be quite rude to him, actually. Perhaps if I'd known he was a necromancer, I wouldn't have been. Perhaps if I'd known, I'd have run screaming with the accusation straight to the Prince-Bishop, and Lorenz would have been burned, and I would have lived and grown and died a charming German girl in a charming, if murderously paranoid, German town.

As it was, I remember weeping into my knees in a cold cell in the dead of night, awaiting trial and execution for the charge of malicious necromancy. I lifted my head as I heard his voice again, laughing. "Oh, sweet Babelin. This is too rich."

"Lorenz?" I reached for the bars, tears still on my face, as I peered up into the darkness. "What are you doing here?" I couldn't keep a note of hope out of my voice. He had a bit of wealth and influence, and I'll admit I'd have given in to him if it would have kept me out of the fire. It wouldn't have, though, I know now. Wealth and influence didn't keep any poor body from that so-called purge.

"I've come to claim you," he said, reaching down out of the dark to pin one of my hands to the bar. I knelt in uncertain silence, and still in hope. "You see, dear Babelin," he laughed, "you'll be mine after all. One way or another." His hold tightened, and I felt my flesh go unnaturally cold. I couldn't move.

"Blood's life, dance," he whispered, and white-hot pain shot through my veins. I must not have screamed, for no one came running. I feel that I must have writhed, but I really can't remember. From there, it's all a fever-dream of necromantic horror. There was blood—mine and some other. There had to be screams, I'd swear there were. I might have been made to drink something. There were sensations I'd never experienced before in life, nor have I known since. I woke thinking it a dream breathed into my lungs by the devil himself. It was the second-worst pain I've ever known.

The worst pain, of course, was the burning the next day. I presume to say that no one has suffered more than me in burning at the stake, for I lived through the entirety. I screamed, then, and screamed, and screamed, until I realized that the pain had finally gone. Assuming myself dead, I fell silent. I slumped perfectly still, bones among the flames,

The Dark Siren

staring up at the lovely red-stone cathedral towering above me. The golden Madonna waved down from her spire as she watched me.

She'll know, I thought quietly, staring up at the figure. *Gott im Himmel, You know that I am Your humble servant, and no necromancer.* And so, peacefully, I waited for my soul to leave my body, to ascend with the smoke into heaven. I waited as they drew my skeleton from the ashes and piled it into a cart with the others. I waited as the cart wheeled out of town. I waited as they dumped us into a rubbish pile, feeling a flare of resentment for the denial of a Christian burial. Well, no matter, I thought. God would know me. Night fell. I waited.

I began to fear. This wasn't hell—it was too mild and peaceable for that—but it wasn't heaven, either. What if neither existed? What if death was sitting in your skeleton, staring at the sky? I wondered if all the skulls beside me had the same growing terror trapped inside. Suddenly, I was glad to have missed that Christian burial after all.

Then Lorenz was there, searching through the bodies. I remembered my nightmare, and if I'd still had blood, it would have gone cold. "Here you are," he said, setting his hands on me. He sounded anxious. Then, "Hah! Yes. No mere corpse, you. Your life and soul remain, and you may yet be animate, with a bit more work. Last night's was an experiment in haste, I'm afraid. Let's get you home, little Babelin."

And so began a new age. I spent less than a year as his thrall. I wonder if I'd have gotten my other senses back if I hadn't killed him so soon. Of course, if I'd waited, he might have gotten even more tired of my rebellious fits and stripped my life or soul away from me. He ought to have done sooner. They're always too sure of themselves, necromancers. Just because they can control the dead doesn't mean they can't be easily made to join them. All the dark powers Lorenz wielded didn't stop me slamming a shovel down on his head when his back was turned. Perhaps he didn't think spicy-sweet little Babelin Göbel would commit murder. Perhaps she wouldn't have, but being a skeleton changes a person. I had already been burned at the stake for necromancy once. What were they going to do—hang me?

"Oh, sure, sure," I say into the phone, spinning the cigar between my thin-gloved fingers. "No problem. When would be a good time for me to call back?"

I still sound like her. Less southern German, more Chicago American, by now, having spent some time in between sounding quite Parisian, then several breeds of Londoner, but the voice has remained with me through it all, the only remainder of that pretty nineteen-year-old girl—excepting, of course, her actual remains.

The Dark Siren

At last, I call my workday a wrap and make for the living room. I don't have to work overmuch. The lack of a grocery bill and the minimal utility bill really cut down on a number of my expenses, and I've made some investments that have paid off over the past scores of decades. The house, the cigars, clothes, nice furniture, books and movies—everything I own falls under the category of "luxuries" for me, and I've been able to build up a few in my time here.

I settle down on the leather recliner, grab the remote, and bring up Netflix. Sight, sound, and story. I still have the capacities to enjoy all three, and doing so helps ground me in my humanity.

Yeah, I still consider myself human. A human soul, bound to a human skeleton, is a human being. I didn't think of it that way, at first. I, like everyone else at that place and time, thought an animate skeleton could only be a monster. I ran much, and hid often, trying to keep away from people. I didn't need water or food, shelter or sleep. I felt the cold, but the discomfort was dim and distant. I thought I could keep hidden forever.

But I was still human after all, and still had the ever-vexing human need for community. It was lonely, the dark and sleepless nights, the endless days without story or song for company. So I found my way to the fringes of humanity once more. My experiences from those times, mincing my way across Germany and France, were harrowing. I tried disguises, but none were long or easily maintained. It was as might be expected—hiding and fear, hatred and damage, flight in the night, screams and cries of "Demon!" and "Thrall!" But there was also kindness, and care, and good people. Those, too, are everywhere, if one looks hard enough.

After about sixty years, the high paranoia was dying down, and I found that big cities, with their constant flow of new and different peoples and ideas, were the safest places for me. I still had to be careful—I have to be careful to this day—but city life let me begin feeling a bit human again. I even made some friends through the centuries. In 1818, a couple of those friends wanted to forge new lives in the infant country across the ocean, and I tagged along in a cargo crate.

I found my way to necro-friendly Chicago not too long before the American Civil War, and I've been making it my home since. In all honesty, I'd rather not live in a necro-friendly anything, considering that my history with their kind has been anything but friendly, but there are two major draws. First, if they're against necromancers, they're against necros' monsters, and I might find myself battered and ripped limb from limb.

The Dark Siren

Second, if I do find myself ripped limb from limb, as has happened more often than I'd like to recount, I've got to pick up the pieces and find a member of that damnable profession. They don't know quite how I was made—apparently Lorenz was something of an innovator, binding life and soul to bone—but they can patch me back together. A few of my bones have been replaced, which feels as weird as it sounds for somewhile, but give it a decade and I can't tell the difference.

Ah, here we go. Time for a classic-horror binge. I've seen most of the big titles that have been released since the beginning of film—sight and sound and story, remember, I'm all for it—and I've found in myself an ironic love of the horror genre. Maybe I find some slight satisfaction in the fact that plain old humans are the monsters every bit as often as the monsters are. Or maybe I like to be comfortably spooked by either kind.

Outside, the dim and cloudy day has become a dark and stormy night. A wind-whipped deluge at my roof and windows compete with the movie streaming on my flat screen for audibility. I tap my remote's volume button to give the film the edge. The weather's rebuttal is a white-out flash of lightning, complete with a burst of thunder I can feel shuddering through the floor and a shrill cry of, "*I hate him!*"

Danielle E. Shipley and Tirzah Duncan

My recliner's leather squeaks with my startled jump. A disembodied soul stands in the television's glow.

"Kid!" I scramble for the remote and pause the show. "What are you—"

"He's awful!" the boy sobs, flickering in and out of opacity. "He won't let me do *anything*. Not read his spell books over his shoulder, not play inside his practice corpses, *nothing*!"

"The killjoy," I say, as Kid flings himself onto my lap. His weight is no more than a press of warm air.

He sniffles. "We *used* to kill things *together*."

I pat at his head. "I'll bet those were the days."

"Well, just the one thing," he amends. "When we didn't want to be Mistress Barbara's assistant anymore. It was barely better than being a thrall. She never let us do anything, either." He scowls tearfully up at me. "He's just like her."

Mistress, hmm? Maybe Kid's mother, more probably his abductor. Stories of toddlers with the potential for death magic kidnapped by necros who sense their gift make the ten o'clock news go round.

"So you killed her," I say, unsure how I feel about this discovery of our common ground.

"*He* did," Kid corrects me. "He separated us first, to make sure he'd have enough power to sing her heart into

The Dark Siren

stillness. Soul stripping's not easy, you know," he says matter-of-factly. "People die from it, if they lose hold of their soul before the spell's complete."

I nod. "I've heard that. Don't most necromancers bind their soul somewhere for safekeeping, though? An amulet, a false tooth, Grandmother's vase?"

Kid lifts his chin defiantly. "I didn't want to be bound. And he didn't use to mind having me around, back when we were both ten. Then he grew up and became the Dark Siren and decided that I'm too little to matter." His chin ducks back down, his shoulders hunched unhappily. "He doesn't even want me there on Hellgate Day."

There's one my calendar shied away from mentioning. "Hellgate Day being ...?"

"It will be our anniversary," he pouts. "Ten years, tomorrow, since we— Wait, what time is it?"

I bring up the TV's display, revealing the night's encroachment on four a.m.

"Never mind," Kid says. "Ten years, *today*, since we split into two. He says that makes it a fitting day to open the hellgate and sing death to the world."

"*What!*"

"Oh, *you* don't need to worry about it," Kid assures me. "You'll be fine. At least, I think you'll be fine ..." His brow puckers, his eyes on me suddenly uncertain. "*Will* you be fine? You are a skeleton, after all."

"Yes," I say tightly, "but the world to be sung death isn't. What exactly is the hellgate, Kid?"

He blinks. "A gate to hell."

So. Just what it sounds like.

"Living souls go in, dead bodies come out," he singsongs, his voice becoming less his own by the note. Becoming the voice that once crooned chills down my spine in the park. The voice of the Dark Siren. "*At the full of the sun, he'll call up a legion of thralls—a symphony of utter darkness, his to conduct until there is no music but his.*"

Bad, bad, very bad. My first instinct is get ahold of the police, the National Guard, anybody trained to handle this kind of crisis. My second instinct is to knock the first instinct silly. Maybe the professionals rush in and apprehend the Dark Siren before he causes too much damage, maybe they don't. All hell's gonna break loose either way if it gets out that a necromancer tried to doom us all.

It'll mean international panic—another great necro-scare sweeping the globe with fire. My bones are living proof of what happens when innocent people get caught between death magic and mundane hysterics. It won't happen again. Not if I can nip it in the bud by taking out the hellgate threat quietly.

The Dark Siren

I push myself from my chair, through the child on my lap, and to my feet. "Where?"

"The Trail of Tears," Kid says, sounding the sweet, playful flute once more. "Lots of death energy there."

"Yeah, I'll bet," I say darkly. The Trail of Tears covers a lot of ground, from as far east as Georgia to as far west as Oklahoma—the distance the contemptible Indian Removal Act of the early nineteenth century forced tens of thousands of Cherokees and other natives from their homes. Close to one in four died as a result. One of the casualties, a Choctaw medicine man, was a personal friend of mine.

"Though, of course, it's all spread out," Kid continues, "so he'll have to consolidate the energy into one spot to form the hellgate." He adds with some pride, "A lesser necromancer couldn't hope to manage such a feat."

"Any idea where on the Trail he plans to do his consolidating?" I ask, my gloved hand going for my smartphone and stylus.

"In between two of the routes, actually. In Shawnee National Forest."

A quick app check later, and I've got a road map from my northern Illinois metropolis to the designated forest at the state's southern end. Barring bathroom breaks (don't need 'em) and awful traffic (unpredictable), I can get within the hellgate's general area in five to six hours. As for the exact location of a gathering of death energy, I'll need a necromantic guide.

I turn back to find my first choice out of sight and my recliner's footrest kicking out and in to the tune of familiar giggles.

"Kid."

He pokes his head out of the seat cushion, his grin an impish gleam.

What I wouldn't give for facial features right now. It's hard for a skull to look anything but gruesomely amused. "I didn't think you could actually touch anything."

"Dead things, I can," he sings merrily. "And leather. Will you give me your gloves so I can use the remote? I want to pick a movie!"

"Nope. Movie time's over. I'm filling my gas tank for a drive to the woods. We've got 'til when, again?"

"The full of the sun," he repeats. "High noon."

I haven't sworn in such expressive German in a long time. "Come on, Kid, we've got to move!"

In this darkest of hours, his little face lights up painfully bright. That's probably the closest he's felt to wanted since even before his body outgrew him.

**

"Looks like this is as far as the roads will get us." Stepping out of the car, I press my fingers to my teeth in an

The Dark Siren

imagined kiss, then tap it to the old station wagon's roof. "Stay safe out here."

"I'll do my best," Kid pipes anxiously. "You keep safe, too."

Maybe I won't tell him I was talking to my car. "You're not coming?"

He shakes his head with vigor, dark bangs seeming to flutter. "Didn't I tell you? The hellgate sucks in *souls*. I'm a soul, and with no body to anchor me. If it opened up, I'd go flying straight into it. Better I keep back."

"I have a soul, and only part of a body. What happens to me if the hellgate opens underfoot?"

Kid wavers like a heat mirage. "I'm not sure. The hellgate's force will try to rip your soul right out of you, leaving your body empty and enthralled, of course."

"Of course," I murmur.

"But it wouldn't be instant. And what with necromantic magic being used to seal your soul, it would probably have a harder time ripping it away than with humans."

"I am human," I growl, then shake my skull. "Never mind. I see your point."

I open my jacket to make sure I've got all of my ammo. Two silenced Smith and Wesson .45s rest ready in hip holsters, with full backup magazines hiding everywhere I could fit them, and a tanto-edged combat knife in case all else fails.

Centuries have rolled by, but necromantic arrogance remains the same. I'll bet my bullets this Dark Siren hasn't got anything in place to stop them.

"So. Which way to the hellgate?"

The soul cocks its head, pointing. "It's that way, but I'm not sure how far."

I set my hands on my hips, looking off into the trees. I don't see any trailhead there. "That way. Great. Who needs a GPS when they've got the soul of Kid?"

"Don't be mean," Kid pouts, sinking halfway down into the ground.

Rubbing my skull, I sigh. "Right. Sorry. But is there any way you could point it out on a map or something?" I proffer the one the ranger gave us on entry.

"Nooooo," he says sadly. "I remember that this is the right area, and I can sense the gathering of death, quite strongly, that way." He looks down. "I can lead you farther. I'll take you until we're a straight shot from the site, but then I'm coming back here."

I pat the area his shoulder seems to occupy. "Thank you, Kid. That's very brave of you."

"It is," he agrees, striking a tragic face. "I risk my utter doom."

The Dark Siren

Failing to turn a laugh into a cough, I tell him to get on with it.

I follow the soul through the underbrush at as quick a pace as I can sustain. A croaking caw draws my gaze up into the trees. A massive raven tilts its head at me, two others strutting along branches. I don't like the birds. I guess I've got a thing against beings that are drawn to death and the dead.

Apparently they don't like me either. Wheeling to branches in front of me, they start up a croaking racket.

"Get off," I snap up at them, feeling my vertebrae tingle. "I might look dead, but there's nothing here for you."

"Uh-oh," Kid singsongs, floating towards them. "I think—"

The three dive as one, wings spread as they swoop towards me. Throwing myself back out of the way, I draw a gun in one hand and the knife in the other, loosing rounds into the creatures. I'm sure I hit, but undeterred, they drop onto me, claws and beaks ripping at my coat. I slice and stab and shoot again, but they keep attacking, one with a whole wing blown off.

"Go for their tongues!" Kid's voice pipes over the ruckus. "Or blow their heads off!"

What in the world …? But with no time to question, I throw myself on top of one of the creatures and hack its head off. The body goes limp, the head still writhing on the ground, beak clacking. Another beak snaps at the back of my spine and I whirl, stabbing the creature through the chest to pin it. Shoving my gun into its open beak, I fire, and the animal crumples as it should, too-large wings spread open.

I look around for the third one and see it writhing in the air, Kid's arms wrapped tight around it. "I've got it, I've got it," the soul says breathlessly as I duck a stray wing clip. "Get its tongue!"

Darting forward, I jam the gun into the corvid's beak and fire. Shuddering, the bird collapses like the other. "How could you hold onto it?" I ask Kid, panting, but I reach the answer even before he speaks.

"It was dead."

"Right," I gasp. "So ... *tongues?*"

"That's where he likes to seal the life to the body," Kid explains. "The Dark Siren. He'll have set the ravens up to keep meddlers away while he works."

"I see." I straighten. "Will there be more of these?"

"Oh, probably absolute *loads*. Flapping, flying flocks of undead *hordes*."

I can't tell if he sounds apprehensive or eager. Just plain dramatic, I decide. "You might have mentioned them before," I note, striding forward with renewed haste.

"I didn't think of it."

The Dark Siren

"Right. At least only my clothes are in danger." I scowl at the tears in the fabric. I can't say that I'm pleased about them. Everything I wear is specially tailored, and none of it cheap.

"Unless there are enough of them. They're strong, clever birds, even dead," he says, sounding much too familiar with the subject. "They'll probably try to tear off your bones at the joints."

"How unkind of them," I murmur, tapping my knife thoughtfully against my jawbone. "I shall have to take care."

Not fifteen minutes of woodland tramping have passed before another band of undead scavengers begins a racket. About forty of them stand in the trees in our path, shrugging their shoulders and turning their beady, death-glazed eyes on us.

"The first lot were meant to turn away wanderers," Kid says conversationally. "These are probably meant to ensure absolutely that they get no further. We're definitely on the right path!"

"Wonderful," I say, and blow one of the creature's heads off. The woods become an explosion of glossy black feathers, furious caws, and even more furious claws and beaks. If I were a flesh creature, I would be blind and bleeding from scores of cuts. As it is, I would be rendered helplessly pinned, but for Kid's presence.

Danielle E. Shipley and Tirzah Duncan

The young necromantic soul swirls an almost giddy circle around me, beating back the thrashing mass of lifeless birds. I'm still beset and buffeted, but he gains me enough breathing room—so to speak—for me to lay into the creatures, shooting their heads off. I can hardly aim for their tongues, but a well-placed hollow-point bullet leaves little enough connecting the tongues to the rest of their bodies, and both fall to the ground.

I can't say how long the battle takes—too long, at my best guess—but sixty-some bullets later, forty bird carcasses lie lifeless *and* motionless on the forest floor. I'm practiced, not perfect.

"Thanks, Kid," I gasp, picking up dropped magazines from among the clacking beaks and twitching partial heads. I'm inclined to mercy-kill the disturbing things, but even if such is possible, I haven't got the time.

"How many more of these do you think there are?" I ask the kid as he giggles his way through the bodies, lifting one or another.

"Don't know," he says, dropping a bird and twirling urgently. "Hurry, hurry, I have to get away from here before noon. Come on, we're close!"

"Close" is apparently forty-five minutes, two distal bones, and all of my ammunition later. Swearing, I find and tuck away my fingertips, then double-check all of my

The Dark Siren

pockets. "I should have started using the knife sooner," I growl, but it's mostly irritation. As the last few minutes and some extreme finger distress have demonstrated, it's no fast or easy task to pin down a raven long enough to behead it.

What I really wish is that I'd saved at least a magazine or two for the Dark Siren himself. One gets a little too caught up in the moment, when fighting countless flying thralls of darkness, to remember to bullet-count. I'm going to have to confront the Dark Siren face-to-skull. Or back-to-skull, if I'm lucky. I can move very quietly when I want to.

"He's straight on from here," Kid whispers, pointing. "In a clearing. It's almost time; all the death he needs has already congregated. I've got to get back. Good luck, Living Skeleton!"

I hope his directions are as straightforward as they seem. I can't afford to get lost now, with all my sense of direction having flown away on hundreds of dark, malevolent wings. "Dead ahead," I whisper to myself, grinning a default grin at my own wordplay, and move quietly through the trees.

It's scant minutes before I hear the singing. The sound sends a shiver up my spine. Eerie, rising and falling, the semi-Latin incantation takes me back to memories of the end of an old life, of Lorenz, of blood's life dancing in a cold, dark cell. Lorenz, however, had no such voice. This sound is ten kinds of beautiful, each more horrible than the last. The Dark Siren deserves his name.

Hastening towards the song—I'm unlikely to be heard over the gruesome aria—I steady my gloved grip on the long knife. The forest around me begins to grow dark, even as the sun reaches towards its zenith, and deeper night seems to fall with every step.

Then I see him. The Dark Siren stands, arms flung out, body shrouded in a dark cloak. His face is an older version of his soul's—pale, beautiful, enraptured. Silky black hair hangs down his back, and I can't tell where it ends and where begin the tendrils of shadow that twine around him. The whole scene is bathed in a pulsing green light, the only light in the glade, emanating from the air before him.

The hellgate, I assume—or else an aurora borealis sung down out of the sky and concentrated in an upright oval before the singing necromancer. I'm going with the hellgate.

Holding my hand down by my side, I try to hide the knife casually behind my femur. As if when someone turns around and sees a skeleton creeping up on them, they're not automatically going to assume they're in danger.

Closer, I can see an arrangement of native artifacts at his feet. I recognize them as belonging to the various tribes forced on the Trail of Tears. Not all of them are sacred, but every one is meaningful, and my bones ache with fury at

The Dark Siren

their use in this evil idiocy—fury at the use of the Trail's deaths. This is really exploitation upon exploitation. Just the sort of thoughtlessness I would expect of a soulless white male necromancer bent on loosing the horrors of hell.

His song suddenly sweeps upward, his voice ringing with triumph, and I let out a startled breath. It's almost complete. The surface of the hellgate shimmers, swells. Deciding stealth is of lesser importance, I begin to race across the meadow, knife raised and ready. Then I feel it. A pull, drawing me on even faster. It wants my soul. The hellgate bulges, and out bursts a rotting human form, groaning in signature undead fashion. The gate bubbles, its edges creeping outward, and more corpses lurch out after the first, pouring to either side of the Dark Siren. His song ends, his laugh now rising high and delighted, sounding disturbingly like Kid's.

Not today. Letting the hellgate's drag on my soul-bound body pull me on, I leap towards the man, only to have a thrall lunge awkwardly into my way. We slam into one another, falling in a tumbling roll towards the necromancer's feet.

He turns, looking down through the shadows that pool and twist around him. "Strange," he says, voice gorgeous, as he peers at us. "Do as I said. Go. Feast." He smiles, dark eyes shining. "Get up, feast on this world and its life. Good thralls, now. Be about your business."

The corpse is trying to clamber on top of me, rotted fingers groping, gaping maw swinging down towards me. I bring my knife up and slam it down into said maw, spiking through its tongue. The creature falls limp, and I yank the weapon around to slash at the necromancer's legs.

I catch only shadow as the Dark Siren steps delicately back. "Ah, how could I have mistaken you, in all this death? It seems my dear deadlings knew better." He tsks. "A living skeleton. You must be the kid's newest find. Oh, and I see you have not only life, but soul. Pity."

He could hardly have missed it. On hands and knees, I've been scrabbling desperately against the hellward slide. I slam my blade down into the ground, anchoring myself. Why didn't I just save one damned magazine? *Sacre bleu*, but I hate ravens!

"I should have liked to study you more closely. A life-to-bone binding is rather inventive." He crouches down, petting the shifting darkness. "Do you know how it was done?"

For a moment, I wish I could spit in his eye. Then I see it—necromantic arrogance. It might save my life once again.

"Bits and pieces," I grit out. "I remember the first thing he said." One hand hiding under me, I begin to work my

The Dark Siren

fingers into the earth, digging down. They might be a downright curse when it comes to anything touchscreen related, but the sharp hardness of my digits comes in useful now and again.

"What's that, then?" he asks, his soulless eyes searching my eyeless sockets.

"Blood's life, *dance*," I say, yanking my blade out of the ground and, with a swift twist, up under his chin. He blinks once, in composed beauty, and I rip downward across his throat. The composure slides away, leaving his face gaping along with the gushing wound. Then, blank-eyed and still sickly beautiful, he rises.

"No. Oh, hell no."

He makes no reply, only turning away from me with a gurgle and a lurch. A Choctaw drum spins away at his clumsy kick, spattered with the blood he trails behind him. Stepping straight through the artifacts, he shuffles along with the other corpses, away from the still-expanding hellgate. The twining darkness stays, swimming across the ground where he left it.

Of course. I curse myself for fifty fools. Have I learned nothing over three hundred years? I killed him, all right—right in his own shadows of enthrallment. He'll only be able to wreak the havoc of a single undead thrall—but the hellgate stands open, vomiting the rotting dead and sucking in souls. And it's still getting bigger.

I slam my knife back into the ground, trying to haul myself away from the pulsing green. A corpse trips over me on its way out, falling to the ground, and I stab its tongue in a fit of frustrated rage. I carried on about the arrogance of the necromancers, but what about my own? Thinking I know enough about necromancy to stop such a powerful one, when I've avoided learning anything more about the arts that made me than whatever's been thrust upon me? Why should the Dark Siren have feared death, when only an idiot would have tried to kill him without first getting him to close the gates of hell?

Should I do something with the artifacts? An artifact myself, I'm reluctant to destroy such things, and far more inclined to see them returned to wherever they belong, but if it might close the hellgate … No, even if I could reach them, I don't know whether their destruction would fix the mess or fix the gate wide open.

The gate's pull seems to strengthen by the moment, my grip in danger of slipping at any one of them. And then, to my horror—not to mention confusion—the Dark Siren reappears at the edge of the clearing. What's brought him staggering back, one hand clamped over the tear in his throat, his gaze unmistakably on me?

The Dark Siren

"Hold on, Living Skeleton!" he calls, voice strained and struggling but music nonetheless. "I can save you! I think."

Not that I knew the guy long, but that doesn't seem like anything the Dark Siren would say, never mind a brain-dead thrall. I look on in renewed hope as the necromancer sings an incantation. Though a word here and there sounds stumbled over, and many a note falls short of its pitch, the orphaned shadows writhe to rejoin with the singer, the rhythm of the gate's light doing the same. A grunt of distress from behind alerts me to a corpse, only its upper body and one leg visible, the rest trapped on the side of the underworld. I could sing, myself, for joy. The hellgate is closing.

Another few measures of the death song, and every thrall in sight collapses to the ground, inanimate once more. The pull on my bones lessens until I can finally crawl farther out of its reach. By the time I'm at the singer's side, the hellgate has faded away to nothing, and noon's light retakes the clearing.

The necromancer drops to his knees. "That all but drained me," he rasps pitiably. "I felt I should be torn asunder and forever damned."

"But you weren't," I say, clapping a hand to his shoulder. "You did good, Kid. Thank you."

The Dark Siren's mouth draws into a grin, the expression still fixed in place when the young soul steps out of the body, leaving it to slump to the ground like the rest of the thralls. The shadows of death magic follow him like affectionate cats as he skips a victory dance around me. "You're welcome!" he pipes. "And that's 'Dark Siren' to you. The body is dead; long live the soul! His power is mine, all mine, hehe!"

I cringe. That is way too strong a necromantic force to let go unsupervised. High time a morally responsible adult took charge of this child. And who knows—maybe that adult's got something to learn about navigating necromancy. You won't catch me napping the next time someone tries to open wide a hellgate.

"Looks like you and I've got some continuing education to do." I reach into the pocket with the raven-displaced bone bits. "Starting with a 'how to' on skeletal repair. I like to maintain my seventeenth-century originals, when possible."

"The seventeenth century?" The little soul gapes. "You're ancient! How on earth have you lasted this long?"

From out of the pocket, I stick an unlit cigar between my teeth. "Clean living."

Petri Parousia
by Matthew Hughes

This story has previously appeared in The Magazine of Fantasy and Science Fiction, February 2008, pp. 83-92.

A research scientist is someone who cannot rest content within the confines of existing knowledge, but always itches to know what is over the horizon.

Or it's somebody who doesn't know to leave well enough alone.

Either definition would fit Wally Applethorpe. So it was natural for him to stay on at Yale medical school on a research fellowship, while I couldn't wait to get out and start cutting people open to give them new knees and hips and other useful parts in return for a six-figure income.

In our last year together, Wally had gotten interested in DNA. Nothing wrong with that, of course. There are plenty of useful things to do with DNA, from catching serial killers to editing congenital diseases out of the gene pool. I suppose you can even make a case for the idea of "improving" the species by making people stronger or more germ resistant, or whatever he was getting up to in his lab over behind the redbrick Farnham Building.

Matthew Hughes

I admit, I could never totally fit my mind around what he was doing. If I could have, maybe I wouldn't have become a surgeon. To me, the human body was not a quasi-metaphysical mystery to be unraveled. It was a kind of soft machine whose parts could be repaired when they broke down, or—even better—be replaced entirely with materials God would have used if He'd only had access to Teflon and stainless steel.

But to Dr. Wally Applethorpe, full-weight genius and Bentham Research Fellow Extraordinaire, the human being was an infinite series of nesting boxes, like those wooden Russian dolls, one inside another. As soon as he got one open, he'd discover another, smaller one inside, and he'd get busy trying to find his way in, world without end.

I moved up to Boston, joined an existing medical group as their bone man, and got busy in my own way: marriage, mortgage, membership in a decent country club. I received regular e-mails from Wally—"Keeping in touch" was always the subject header—to which I replied as briefly as I knew how. You may not know many real geniuses, but let me tell you: close up, over the long term, they can truly get on your nerves.

Then, late one morning, he showed up at my office. Sharon, the receptionist, was still buzzing me to ask if I wanted to receive an unscheduled visitor when he walked right through my door and said, "Jimmy-boy, you've got to see this."

By reflex, I said, "Don't call me Jimmy-boy. It's Jim, or James, or what the hell, Dr. Feltham."

He gave me that look he always used to give me, the *Let's not make a big deal out of nothing* look (although it seemed to me his whole life was about making big deals out of next to nothing), and said, "I've got to show you this!"

Now, someone who didn't know Wally Applethorpe might think that the logical response to his statement would be, "What?" But I'd spent three years in a grungy New Haven apartment with him, so my question was, "Why?"

He blinked, and put on that expression of astounded innocence that went with the clear blue eyes, perpetually pink cheeks, and shock of corn-yellow hair. "Because you're my friend," he said.

"I'm not your friend, Wally," I said. "I'm just a guy who wound up rooming with you because I couldn't find anything cheaper. Why don't you try to think of us as strangers who got stuck in an elevator and then happily went their separate ways?"

At which he gave me his *You old kidder, you* look and launched into the matter that had brought him here. "Give me some blood," he said, pulling a specimen kit out of his pocket.

This time, my response was the same as anybody's would have been. "Why?"

"So I can show you what I've been doing."

"Why?"

He sighed indulgently. "'Cause you're going to want to get in on the ground floor of this. I'm launching a company, got some backers, going to make some big buckazoids, do a lot more research. Sky's the limit. So naturally I thought of my old buddy, Jimmy-boy."

It was on the tip of my tongue to say, "I'm not your old buddy," but another part of my brain weighed in and said to me, *Just 'cause he's an annoying little twerp doesn't mean he isn't brilliant. How many people could stand Bill Gates before he was a multi-billionaire?*

I rolled up my sleeve, and he efficiently took twenty cc's out of me. "Now what?" I said.

"I'll be back tomorrow," he said, "to show you."

"That's kind of a long commute from New Haven."

"Didn't you get my e-mail?" he said. "I'm just six blocks from here now. Hey, you free for lunch?"

I pleaded an urgent, though imaginary, consult with Jag Sharma, our geriatrics specialist. And, thank God, I did genuinely have a couple of hip replacements scheduled for the afternoon, which allowed me to ease him out the door while he was still bubbling about how it was just like the good old days, the two amigos back in the saddle again. But after he had gone, I wondered how I would keep him at a manageable distance.

I went out front to plot strategy with Sharon. "What a sweet guy," was her opening comment, which was just what girls always said about Wally. Of course, they hadn't had him at full strength and close quarters for three years. Or maybe it was just me. Either way, and notwithstanding the puzzled look she gave me, I worked out a system with Sharon: she would buzz me the moment she saw Wally out in the elevator lobby and heading for the glass doors. That would give me time to get into somebody else's office and close the door before he could inflict himself on me at will. With Wally, I had found that control was the key to maintaining sanity.

But, of course, he was beyond control; so the system failed on its first test. Impatient with the slowness of our elevators, Wally came up the fire stairs and was past Sharon and halfway to my office before she could buzz me with the code words, "Mrs. Arkwright to see you."

So Wally caught me, my desk spread with insurance forms, which meant I couldn't plead any urgencies to justify shortening his visit. He had brought along a small plastic case, like an insulated lunch box, from which he removed a set of Petri dishes with transparent covers. They were marked with numbers and names. The names were familiar.

"What is this?" I said.

He touched one of the covers. Its label read Stanley Feltham. "That's your granddad," he said.

Next to it was a dish labeled Rose (Maguire) Feltham. "And your grandma."

The two other dishes were labeled with the names of my mother's parents.

"What is this?" I said again.

"I've isolated each of your grandparents' DNA," he said, giving me that wide-eyed, farm-boy look that meant he had cracked open another doll.

"How?"

So now, finally, he explained. He could unravel a subject's DNA to separate what each of that person's parents had contributed to the mix. It involved microlasers and several kinds of enzymes—cutters, movers, and assemblers, he called them—and the whole process was handled by a super-fast computer that could sort through all the possible combinations and find the one that was true.

"I patented the process, and we're going public in a few weeks," he said. "Write me a check for five grand and I'll give you stock warrants that will be worth two percent of the company."

Petri Parousia

"And what will the company be worth?" I said.

"Why, billions," he said.

"Why?" I said. "What will people do with their grandparents' DNA?"

He shrugged. "I suppose some of them will put it into an egg, insert it into a womb, and give birth to grandma or grandpa. Most people have fond memories of their grandparents—from childhood, that is—but by the time the kids are old enough to really get to know them, the old folks are getting ready to shuffle off this mortal coil. Or they're senile."

"Okay," I said, and thought about it. My mother's parents had died before I was born, and the world would thank me for not creating another Stan Feltham: there was already an oversupply of sourpusses. "Supposing there is a market for grandparent clones. It can't be worth billions."

He waggled his hands on either side his head. "Think, man," he said, then he spread them wide as if offering the whole world. "We're not just talking grandparents. We can go way back. Way, way back."

"How way?"

"Wa-a-a-ay, way."

"Give me a for instance," I said.

He moved the Petri dishes aside and sat on the corner of my desk. "Got any famous ancestors?"

Matthew Hughes

There was a legend in the family on my mother's side that we were descended from one of Benjamin Franklin's illegitimate sons. My mother had never been sure whether she should brag about it or hush it up. I told Wally about it.

"Ben Franklin?" he said. "Really? How come you never mentioned this?"

"I guess it never came up."

I probably had mentioned the Franklin connection at some point, but I wasn't surprised that Wally had missed it. In any discussion, he usually did most of the talking; listening was not among his alpha-level attributes.

"Well," he said, picking up one of the dishes that contained my maternal ancestors, "how'd you like to have Ben Franklin as your own son?"

I thought about it, and he read my face. "And how much would you pay to be able to do that?" he said.

I wasn't actually thinking about me raising a young Ben Franklin. Chances were he would have been a handful and a half. I was thinking about all the people who named their kids Jared or Jessica or some other J-name just because it was that year's fashion. They never thought about what it would be like for the poor kid to be one of four or five identically named people in every group they'd ever join, never thought about how the kid would feel knowing that that most personal of possessions, one's own name, had been chosen merely because it was popular and because their parents were irredeemably shallow.

I was thinking about just how many such people existed and how many of them were willing to spend their bank accounts to remain in vogue. "Should I make the check out to you or the company?" I said.

And so we were in business.

***

And a very good business it was. Wally's company—Ancest, he called it—caught the world's eye and the world's ear. The backers had poured in plenty of start-up money, a good portion of which went into a saturation ad campaign on network television. Within days, Leno and Letterman were making jokes about their imaginary ancestors, Regis and Kelly were interviewing Wally live, and the stock price hit two hundred a share then split. It was structured as a straight-out franchise operation, and the prospective franchisees were fighting each other to get in the door.

"Come work with me," Wally said. He offered me a salary that was one figure more than the six I'd been getting as an orthopedic surgeon, plus options, expense account, corner office, and company Lexus.

I said, "What on earth can I do for you?"

"It's medical research. You're a doctor."

"I'm just a bone cutter."

Matthew Hughes

He gave me his bashful Tom Sawyer look and said, "You're my touchstone. Everybody else, they're always slapping me on the back and telling me what a brilliant researcher I am. You don't do that. You're the only one keeps my feet on the ground, Jimmy-boy."

I should have run for the hills. Instead, I took the corner office with the title of Executive Vice President on the mahogany door, behind which I did a lot of not very much while being well paid for my exertions. It turned out, though, that there was one chore Wally wanted me to take over.

"I'd like you to interface with the backers," he said. "Give me less time in meetings, more time in the lab. I've got some interesting projects on the burners."

"Okay," I said. I figured it wouldn't be too onerous a task to schmooze the money people: dazzle them with a little science and set visions of sugarplum dividends dancing in their heads. Thus armed in my innocence, I walked into the Wednesday afternoon board meeting with a fat folder of glowing results from the first few weeks and even shinier projections for the next three quarters.

"We've blown right through the granddad and granny market, and we're into a serious run on major historical figures," I said. "Now that the federal court has ruled that DNA from more than four generations back is public domain, it's not just Robert E. Lee's descendants who can

Petri Parousia

have him for a son; we estimate we'll sell him to about five percent of the population below the Mason-Dixon Line. Plus, the interest in European monarchs is picking up, particularly the Bourbons."

I had plenty more, but I was strongly sensing that the five men in black suits on the other side of the table didn't give a damn. I set aside the bar charts on eighteenth-century poets and nineteenth-century composers and said, "Gentlemen, am I missing something?"

"Project Parousia," said the Chairman of the Board. He was a big, stone-faced man with eyes that had had a lot of practice at weighing and winnowing his fellow human beings. I had the feeling I was close to being assigned to the giant bin labeled *Chaff*.

I shuffled through my papers, but I knew there was nothing in there about any Project Parousia. I'd never heard of it, although the name rang a faint bell.

"I don't have any information on that project," I said.

"Then get some," said the Chairman. "Or get Applethorpe up here." The other board members nodded, their jaws grimly set, and I realized that they were all cut from the same block of close-grained hardwood as the Chairman. Now that I inspected them closely, I saw that they didn't have the sleek, well-nourished look common to the upper links of the corporate food chain. Instead, each had the aspect of the zealot; they might have been carried over from some previous era when the most popular pastimes were burning witches and crushing heretics under piles of boulders.

"We'll be back tomorrow," he said. "Be prepared to tell us what we want to know."

***

I went down to the lab. It was below ground and behind a number of thick steel doors and an even larger number of men who wore uniforms and sidearms. At the last door, even my senior-executive pass was not enough to get me through, but I managed to convince the head guard to buzz Wally, and he told them to admit me.

When I came into the lab he was bent over the monitor of a scanning electron microscope, humming to himself. Without looking up, he said, "I think we've made it all the way back to Cro-Magnon man. In a week or two, I should be ready to clone a prehuman hominid. After that, Jimmy-boy, I'm going to get some birds and work back toward the dinosaurs."

"What's Project Parousia?" I asked. My teeth chattered a little. The air was chilly; the large room was designed to keep its banks of super-fast computers happy. Humans could put on a sweater.

Petri Parousia

"Oh, just a bee in the board's bonnet," he said, looking up for a moment. "Don't worry about it."

"No bee would survive a second in any bonnet of theirs," I said. "Who are those people?"

He had turned back to his monitor. "Backers," he said. "Money people."

I put a hand on his shoulder and pulled him down to my lowly plane. "No," I said. "They're not. Tell me how you found them."

I could see him consulting the part of his memory where he stored irrelevant details. "I didn't," he said after a moment. "They found me. After I published my paper on retrogressive DNA sequencing, they came to see me."

"It was their idea to set up the company?"

"Uh-huh."

"But they're not interested in our actual results and revenue projections."

He looked mildly puzzled. "They're not?"

"No, the only thing they care about is Project Parousia."

"Hmm," he said, and gestured to a lab bench across the room. "It's over there."

His microscope was pulling him back to wherever he went when he was working, but I exerted a more immediate level of force and pushed him over to the Parousia bench. He examined a series of Petri dishes connected to sensors and probes that were in turn linked to one of the big computers, then checked a stream of data that was zipping across a monitor.

"Almost done," he said. "Of course, it's just fantasy."

"What is?"

"Their idea."

"Tell me about it," I said.

Wally said he figured that the board had gotten themselves all wrapped up in that goofy book about a secret society that had protected the descendants of a union between Jesus and Mary Magdalene through two thousand years. I hadn't read the book, but I had heard about misguided enthusiasts trying to dig up church floors to get at supposed clues.

I saw it now. "They want you to work backwards through the DNA until you've got a clone of Jesus." And now I remembered what Parousia meant. It was Greek for *the Second Coming*.

"They want to bring on the end of the world," I said.

Wally was the only person I'd ever heard use the word "Pshaw." He used it now, then added, "It's just a myth."

"Work with me a moment," I said. "Suppose it isn't a myth. Suppose there really is a secret society. 'Cause I'm thinking if there ever was a secret society of religious fanatics, they'd look an awful lot like our board of directors."

"Still," he said, "what are the chances they could be right?"

"I don't know," I said, "but how much research could you get done if the seas are boiling and we're all being pitched into a lake of fire?"

"That's not going to happen."

"Okay, suppose all you give them is a mild-mannered carpenter—aren't they likely to think you've teamed up with the Antichrist to wreck their plans? 'Cause they don't look like the kind of people who would get their lawyers in and sue. I'm thinking they're more the pitchforks-and-torches kind."

At that moment the Parousia Project's computer emitted a discreet ding. Wally leaned over and picked up the last Petri dish in the series. He peered into it. "There it is," he said, then looked around. "But I don't see any angels or wise men."

"Fine," I said. "Tomorrow I'll give it to them, and maybe they'll go away happy." Though I didn't think so. But planes left for obscure corners of the world every hour, and I would have enough time to pick a good one.

Except that I noticed how Wally was looking at the dish with that expression I'd seen so many times before. He had found another doll he could crack open.

"No," I said, and reached for the dish. "For once, leave well enough alone."

But he had already slipped it back into its connective armature, and his fingers rippled across the computer's keyboard.

He turned to me with that smile of genius I'd seen so often before, the one that is a virtual twin to the grin of madness. "I can prove it's a myth," he said. "You see, if that's really Jesus, the Son of God, then half its DNA is Mary's, and the other half is ..."

Ding went the computer.

Behind him, from the lab bench, a light glowed.

I turned to run, but the floor shook and the walls cracked, and I was thrown down.

I looked up and saw that the Petri dish was enveloped in a flame that burned yet did not consume, and a voice that came from everywhere at once said, "Put off the shoes from thy feet, for the place where thou standest is holy ground."

"Oh, God," I said.

No Time to Lose
by Ariana Tiens
Translated by Kai Herbertz

Darkness …

Rain …

Torrents of water streamed down the window and distorted the view, so that looking at the world outside was barely possible. I strongly hoped that everything went well, that we had been successful with our mission, because if we had not, the world I knew would vanish into thin air in a few weeks.

I should have been there. Instead I stood here and stared out of the loft's windows and was so tense that the room around me seemed to become a vacuum. I paced up and down in front of the window like a caged animal. I stopped again and looked outside.

I heard the elevator door open and whirled around. It was Mary. She stood in the room, and around her a pool of water formed. Drops of water ran down her face and fell from her hair. When she took off her coat to hang it up on the clothes rack I realized that her suit was ripped up in several spots. "It didn't go as planned," she said.

Ariana Tiens

"What does that mean?" As I asked the question I felt my face contort and hoped that Mary would read anger rather than panic. "Where is Stan?" I asked.

Mary began to answer, when the visu-speech activated itself.

You have failed! our employer stated. I felt as if someone had rammed a Taser into my stomach. I felt queasy, because I knew that he was aware of the part of the story that Mary and I were not. The part that was about Stan …

"At first everything went well," Mary defended herself. "We pursued the target to an office building in the financial district, then we secured the floor where the deal went down. The drones were set loose. That the opposition possessed crawlers to locate us was an incalculable risk we weren't prepared for." She stared angrily toward the projection of our employer.

I closed my eyes. "You didn't enable the thermo-cover."

"There were no thermo-scanners on our radar," Mary replied.

I have equipped you and instructed you to prevent the deal. You couldn't finish the job, and the only thing you can do now is save your lives in a dark future. From now on you're on your own. You will be the hunted.

"What about Stan?" I asked again.

No Time to Lose

The image of our employer wavered. He lifted up a newspaper. *Next week he will be found dead. I'm sorry.*

I buried my face in my hands.

So far there is nothing about you. But I doubt that it'll stay like that. Good luck. The visu-speech cut the line.

"I'm getting changed," Mary said coolly. "It's best if you pack your suitcase." With that she went away.

***

It started completely normal, and yet in such a way that it seemed to me back then as if I had gotten into a movie. I had received a job offer from Stanley.

He led a detective agency and said that he wanted to have a psychologist on board. I found everything extremely fascinating and exciting and arrived in his office with a pounding heart. That I could ever work as a detective lay beyond my imagination. That we would all become agents a short while later was inconceivable at this juncture.

Mayne & Partner was written on the office door. Behind the entrance lay an antechamber with a sofa, a table, and two armchairs. Stanley approached me with a smile and greeted me. He bade me to be seated. I sat down on the sofa. Stanley took a seat on an armchair.

"Mary!" he called out. A woman with shoulder-length blond hair, who wore a business suit, appeared in the doorframe of a room that was labeled IT.

Ariana Tiens

She leaned against the wall with her arms crossed. "Do we need a secretary?" she asked and looked at me dismissively.

"May I introduce you," Stanley commented, looking at me. "This is Mary. She is the person that 'partner' refers to, since she is my right hand, so to speak. She knows how to hack e-mail accounts, find out addresses, and even disable alarm systems. But unfortunately she is less savvy when it comes to people, and that's now-and-then essential, if you want to gather information."

Mary kept a straight face when she said: "This is Stanley, by the way, who represents the 'Mayne' and who doesn't even bother to ask 'partner' whether a certain woman would perhaps be one too many for this agency."

Stanley rolled his eyes. "Mary, could you please …"

I wanted to interject something before the situation became too precarious. "I'm sorry that—" However, Mary did not allow me to continue.

"You don't have to be sorry that Stanley claimed we needed help, but if you want to know anything about a person, then look at her PC. And that's something I do best."

"You don't seem to particularly like me," I noted, amused.

No Time to Lose

Mary snorted. "If you need a degree to determine that …" She left the sentence unfinished and smiled in a sarcastic way.

Stanley looked at me. "My apologies. I can explain. I have really—"

"It's all right." I smiled. "You don't have to explain anything. I already know Mary well enough to gage the situation."

"Is that so?" Mary asked, and her eyes twinkled with anger.

I looked her straight in the eyes. "You have a tendency to isolate yourself, strictly work alone, and often alienate people as a result. You are in favor of me leaving, but you don't mention at all that you would leave, if I were to stay. This indicates that you value your job, perhaps, because it is the only one that fits. I'm sorry that you have a problem with me, but you are probably against me, because I am a woman, and you would have less of a big problem if Stanley had brought in another man."

Mary looked away, eager not to let it show that my claims were spot on. Her voice was perfectly calm when she said: "I don't see you as competition, no worries. You're playing in another league, and that's one beneath me."

"You don't see me as competition, but rather as a nuisance." I paused. "Am I in? Or do I have to explain in front of Stanley why you perceive me as a nuisance?" Adrenaline flooded my body. I had the impression that my jeans were glued to the sofa's leather due to sweat gathering at every contact point, but I smiled at Mary.

Mary skulked like a tiger before it pounced. Then she lifted the corners of her mouth. "Okay," she said matter-of-factly to Stanley. "She can stay." Then she turned around and disappeared into the IT room without slamming the door, or any other signs of attitude.

"Wait." Stan looked at me and grinned. "What is it that Mary wants to keep hidden from me?"

"Sorry," I said. "Confidentiality."

That was the first day in the detective agency. Stan welcomed me and asked me to start the very next day at ten. That would be the time when most of the clients came by.

The first week went well. Rather uneventful. Once in a while Stan asked about my opinion regarding a client. While the clients waited outside on the antechamber's sofa, I served coffee and engaged them inconspicuously in conversation. Often I could not find out much in the short amount of time, but I could say whether I had the impression that someone was hiding something or if someone really came in with personal matters. For example, one woman turned out to be the sister-in-law that wanted to spy on her sister's husband.

No Time to Lose

Mary called me into her office within the first three days under the pretense that I should set up my e-mail profile.

"What makes you think that I regard you as a nuisance rather than competition?" she asked. Again, perfectly neutral. I must admit, I liked Mary. It sounds crazy, but she was simply extraordinary. This was what attracted me to psychology. People with psychological issues thought differently from the average person and were therefore often more interesting. Mary did not seem psychologically unstable to me, but she had an air of aloofness. With her blond hair and the masculine clothes that highlighted her cool model's face, she always exuded complete presence whenever she entered the room. She almost never raised her voice, and you never heard her whisper or laugh. Everything she said sounded superior and at the same time slightly bored. As if everything did not concern her.

I tried to dodge the question. "Oh, stop it. I also need a job. What does it matter to you? We—"

"I asked you something," Mary said.

I crossed my arms. "You see me as a nuisance because you probably have an issue with women, in my professional opinion."

"How do you figure?" Mary seemed only marginally interested, not angry.

That puzzled me. I mustered all my courage and declared: "You kept using the gender-neutral term 'partner' instead of switching to a female pronoun, at the very least. In addition, you're wearing men's clothes and work as a hacker, which isn't necessarily typically female. When you met me, you called me 'a certain woman,' which made me conclude that you only reluctantly categorize yourself as a woman. Subconsciously, of course." I started to sweat again. Mary looked at me for a long time.

"I hate shrinks," she said and opened the door so that I could go to the antechamber again.

Stan had just left his office with a client and escorted the man to the door. As soon as the client was gone, Stan regarded me. "You should learn a bit more about detective work," he said and took his jacket from the coatrack. "Come along!"

Shortly thereafter we were outside and sitting in the car. "I'm going to show you how to keep someone under surveillance," Stan said.

"Do I have to?" I wanted to know. I felt uneasy at the thought of following other people.

"It would, if you weren't able to, make no sense to work in a detective agency." We stopped in front of a coffeehouse. He handed me a photo. "That's the target," he explained.

No Time to Lose

A young woman with dark curly hair was shown in the picture. "Does she work in this coffeehouse?" I asked.

"No!" Stan indicated at the other side of the road, a bit farther down. "Rule number one: never work in an obvious way. On Fridays she trains in that gym. We are going to wait until she leaves, and then we follow her. Her car is yellow and parked over there."

For a while we sat there in silence. "What has she done?" I asked.

"She and her husband founded a company. Lately they are often arguing about the company's future. Our client is worried that his wife is going to reach out to the competition and perhaps ruin the company by passing on insider information. We are supposed to find out whether she meets with someone or not. And if so, we are to take photos. Rule number two: in principle we need multiple cars for surveillance. I currently have three cars plus Mary's. Ideally you should memorize the entire city map. I'm going to show you why the—"

"*Is that her?*" I pointed at the gym's driveway. A woman crossed the street.

Stan looked frustrated. "Thanks! Rule number three: never get distracted." The woman got into a yellow convertible and drove off. "You're not bad for a beginner."

Stan smiled. He waited a moment before starting the engine and driving after the woman.

He always remained two or three cars behind her. When she turned into a fast food drive-thru he kept going past. "A good opportunity to show you the rest," Stanley said. He took a key from the glove compartment. He accelerated and drove into a side street. A black car with slightly tinted glass stood there. He parked the car, and we got into the other car. It had a car phone.

"Normally it'd go down like this: I'm driving one car, and Mary drives another. Most of the time she uses her own car. You know how she is."

I smiled.

"If one of us is tailing the target and notices that they are approaching an intersection, then we would inform the other person, and they can take over. If several different people are behind you, then that's normal. If it's always the same guy behind you, then that's suspicious," Stanley explained while starting the engine.

"Where are we going?" I asked.

"At the drive-thru she can only go right," Stanley replied and turned a few corners. "Therefore she'll be here soon," he concluded once we drove on a wider road. Indeed, a short time later the yellow convertible reappeared in our rearview mirror.

No Time to Lose

"It looks like she's going home," Stanley said. "We're taking a break and eating at a bistro nearby."

"I like this job better by the minute," I said.

She lived in a house in the better part of town. The flat was on the third floor, and from our table at the bistro we could see the driveway and the street.

"As of tomorrow, we'll take separate cars," Stanley decided. "Come on!" he murmured and poked me in the side. "It's ideal for beginners with that car." He meant the yellow convertible.

"All right, if you tell me when to drive in what direction …" I said.

"It'll be fine." He winked at me.

"And Mary is going as well?" I asked.

He grimaced. "Yes. I mean, she is doing a really good job. But she is not necessarily discreet. It's not her fault—she's just drawing attention. Not least due to her clothes, her style—"

"Are you saying that my clothes are boring?!" I was indignant.

"Hey!" He lifted his hand. "You women are fantastic at twisting words. I did not mean boring. I meant … low key."

I stared at him in silence and then looked away. I really did not have to listen to this.

Ariana Tiens

From the corner of my eyes I saw him sliding back and forth on his chair. I turned my attention back to my cup of coffee. Stanley's jaw twitched as if he wanted to inhale, but his lips remained pressed together. Finally he did speak.

"I don't know if other people think you're boring. Perhaps you don't get noticed by everyone, but … I noticed you."

I looked over. He regarded me when he added: "Otherwise I would not have wanted you here with me."

It was one of those moments when it is best not to say anything more in order to not spoil them. And that is what we did.

***

"Do you have everything?!" Mary joined me in the room. I had not made much progress packing the suitcase. A few pairs of pants, a few sweaters—when I took the photo of Stanley and me from the nightstand, I had stopped …

"There must be another way," I said resolutely while staring at the picture.

"There is none. The first and last chance was then, and now it's too late," Mary said with an unfamiliar amount of aggression in her voice.

"You are the tech expert. We have access to future technology. Why shouldn't we be able to use it to fight the future that is brewing right now?"

No Time to Lose

"Because the people who are working to darken that future possess even more secret secret weapons. The plane leaves in three hours." She laid a ticket on my nightstand.

"I booked it on your third passport. I will now try to erase all traces." With that she started to walk away again.

"You were always an expert at portending doom and gloom," I said. My larynx seemed to solidify to stone.

Mary had reached the door. "You sound like a child that was told Santa Claus isn't coming because he doesn't exist." She turned to me. Her lips had lost their neutral form. Some emotion apart from indifference and narcissism had snuck on her face. Nothing had shocked me more on this evening.

"You know," she said, "the things we did, we were able to do. You had the intuition, I had the gadgets, and Stanley had the plan. Nobody mastered the art of surveillance and unveiling secrets like we did. But we should have declined this secret-agent business from the start. We should have kept our hands off of the arcane arts. You see it in countless horror movies, but you still go wrong." She seemed to look right through me and eventually turned around. "Good luck," she said and went downstairs.

***

"Mary!" Stanley shouted through the office instead of just going next door.

"What?" Mary shouted back.

"I could use some help here," Stanley shouted.

I looked up from my work. "What's the problem?" I asked and stepped up behind him. "Did your computer crash?" At that point I often sat with him in his office. We were hard to separate …

I frowned.

I am looking for someone who could run investigations that go beyond normal requirements. If you want the job, find out where to meet me. The payment is going to be discussed on site.

"You're aware that this is a joke, right?" I asked, alarmed. Nobody could take that seriously.

"That's what I thought at first, too, but"—Stanley looked at the screen with narrowed eyes—"this e-mail has no sender."

Now I was perplexed. Mary already stood beside the desk, which I only noticed when she said, "No sender?" It sounded less neutral than normal, but rather disdainfully doubtful, as if she meant to say *what did you overlook, you idiot?*

Mary positioned herself in front of the monitor, clicked a few times with the mouse, and suddenly Stan had to jump back, because without saying a word Mary began to sit down.

No Time to Lose

"That's the work mode," Stan said and nodded toward Mary. "Once her curiosity is piqued she is in her element and not responsive anymore. That it piqued her curiosity practically confirms the importance." He snuck around the desk. "Mary, could you perhaps—" The printer started humming, and Stan left his sentence unfinished.

I snatched away the sheet of paper and stared at it. "Did you print the wrong e-mail?"

Stan took the sheet out of my hand. "Hi guys! All the best holiday greetings from Madrid! We're writing an e-mail since we're too lazy to send postcards. We didn't want to keep this picture from you …" Underneath was a photo of two women and one man, who wore sunglasses and carried parasols in front of a white building.

Something sparkled in Stanley's eyes. "So we have an e-mail without a sender that changes its text when you try to print it," he summarized.

Mary jumped up and snatched the printout out of his hand. She looked at it with her always completely cool expression, then she said calmly and stretched out: "Nice."

She sat down once more, and her hands flew over the keyboard.

"Does that mean we have to meet him in Madrid?" I asked and studied the photo that had come out of the printer. In the meantime it was the end of the workday. We were in agreement that this case was too interesting to ignore, even if it turned out to be a professional joke. We did everything in our power to decipher the e-mail.

"Presumably it is not Madrid," Stanley said. "This here"—He tapped the printout in front of me—"is only camouflage. Besides, it would be too easy for someone who kept Mary busy for over two hours."

"Are you sure that it's a man?" Mary asked without taking her eyes off the screen.

"Almost certainly," I answered.

"What do you mean by almost?" Mary kept looking intensely at the monitor.

"You can analyse the gender by looking at the e-mail and the choice of words. I guess that the probability that this is a woman is ten to eleven percent."

"Still high enough." Mary kept hammering the keyboard, and a moment later she quickly hit the tabletop. "Damn it!"

"What happened?" Stan asked, alarmed, and was at the desk in three steps to see if his PC had died.

"I can't get in. This e-mail practically has no sender and was sent from a computer at an Internet cafe. However, it wasn't sent yesterday or today, but …"

No Time to Lose

Mary shook her head, got up, and walked through the room. She took the printout, which lay in front of me on the desk.

"When was it sent?" Stan asked.

"Look at the date," Mary replied.

"When?" I asked Stan, who looked at Mary's results file.

"In one week," Stan said absentmindedly.

All of a sudden the room felt eerily cold …

***

We sat in a car near the Internet cafe. Stan had equipped Mary and me with an in-ear. We wore tiny microphones in our collars.

"You have to be extremely careful. Whoever wants to talk to us is way ahead of us," Stan warned.

"That's exactly why you should stay in the car, Mayne. Otherwise he'll take flight," Mary said.

I laughed, which sounded twice as loud over the car radio speakers.

"I'm serious," Stanley said to me.

"Me too." I looked at him. "I know that this is probably the, let's say, most extreme case we've ever taken, but you know me. I have a knack with people and can cope with strain."

"The guy is a hacker," Mary said. "I'm going in first."

Stanley nodded at her, and Mary downright jumped out of the car. Stanley balanced the laptop on his legs, and we heard Mary's steps as she moved on the sidewalk. Shortly thereafter we heard a doorbell.

"How quaint," Stanley murmured.

I waited a while until Mary had said, "For an hour." And I heard coins rattling.

"The third one, over there," said a person who sounded very young and very tired. Probably a student that took the job because he did not need to handle anything above twenty dollars.

"I'm in, and I'm sitting by the window," Mary whispered a short while later, possibly into her hand.

"Are there any suspicious persons?" Stan asked.

"When Coleen enters she should pay attention to the curly-haired guy who is sitting in the far-left corner. The others are unremarkable."

"Go," Stanley said, and I left the car. I walked along the busy road and entered the cafe.

"Hello. What's the shortest amount of time I can get?" I inquired.

The guy behind the counter looked similar to what I had imagined. Blond unkempt hair and stubble. "Half an hour," he said.

No Time to Lose

"I think that's sufficient," I said and put the money on the counter.

"The one all the way on the right," the cashier said and pointed in that direction. I took the opportunity to look around the room. Mary sat at the window. The computer he had allocated to me was at the other end of the window. Most of the monitors were arranged in front of the window, and there were others in a semicircle along the walls. In the middle of the room stood a pillar with another three computers arranged around it. Many seats were taken. The curly-haired man that Mary had mentioned had thick, dark, curly hair, a three-day beard, and wore sunglasses. Mary could watch him in the window's reflection. Behind me an older man walked up to the counter and addressed the cashier. "Excuse me. Could you help me now? Can I sit over there at a computer? My grandson wanted a picture, so my daughter gave me this thing. That's called USB, right?"

"How adorable!" I chuckled.

"Please concentrate, darling!" I heard Stan's voice via the in-ear speaker.

I sat down at the computer and navigated to a random website with cooking tips.

"I don't know," I whispered while I hid my mouth behind my hand.

"What exactly don't you know?" Stan asked.

Ariana Tiens

I typed "The guy looks too suspicious" into my cell phone and sent the text to Stan.

I looked around. Everywhere were Asians, long-haired gamers playing battle simulations, and girls who chatted.

"Mary says the guy is repeatedly reaching into his briefcase," Stan said.

"Okay," I said at half volume.

I deliberated. It would be best to get up and order a coffee to get another better view, I thought. I got up and walked to the counter. The guy had just come back as the older man continued a speech of thanks with the words "Let's show them that gramps can handle the Internet."

I ordered a coffee and watched the man with the three-day beard.

"Abort!" Stan suddenly shouted, just as I took my cup of coffee. I twitched, and coffee spilled over the edge of the cup.

"What?" I heard Mary ask at half volume and annoyed. Fortunately her monitor showed a load screen at that moment.

"Back to the car," Stan just said.

Shortly thereafter Mary stood up. I finished my coffee and looked up many useless websites, then I also left.

No Time to Lose

"What happened?" I asked when I reached the car and threw myself on the passenger seat. Stan wordlessly handed over the laptop. I saw another e-mail without a sender.

The e-mail was open and read: *If you want to talk to me, you should disable the micro transmitters of the two ladies.*

I gasped. Mary sat on the backseat and looked out of the window with her arms crossed.

Stan turned around to face her. "He found out that you were equipped with transmitters and that you're there together, and he sent two messages without you noticing. How did that guy manage to do that?!"

I also turned to Mary, who remained silent. "Do you think it was the guy in the back on the left?" I asked.

"If I knew anything, I'd answer," Mary said.

All of us were startled when someone banged on the hood of our car. Horrified, we stared at the man, who had appeared next to the car as if out of thin air. I recognized the old man, who had also been at the Internet cafe. When he tapped his collar to signal that the transmitters should be turned off, I noticed that my mouth still stood open. Mary and Stan had already jumped out of the car. I pushed the button to disable the program for the transmitters.

Then I slowly opened the door.

Ariana Tiens

"At least Miss Coleen was smart enough to really disable the transmitters," the man said and looked over to me. "Otherwise you might have lost the job."

"Why don't you introduce yourself first? Who knows whether we even want to take your job? And if you've got work for us, why play such games?" Stan positioned himself in a defensive stance.

"If you didn't want the job, you wouldn't be here," the man countered. "If you need to have a name for me, then you can call me One. Everything else weren't games, but tests. You have passed. There is no need for introductions. You are Stanley Mayne, Mary Sanders, and Coleen Kremer. You are the best private eyes of this decade. If you want to know more about this task, we have to drive a few blocks. Then I'll explain it to you. This spot isn't safe enough."

"No problem," Mary said and showed the hint of a menacing smile. "He's sitting with me."

If I had been in One's stead, I would have been scared.

We drove to an abandoned factory nearby.

"Please stop," One said.

It was strange to call a man that, but this guy was unreal enough to be satisfied with a number for a name.

"How exactly did you pull that off with the e-mail?" Mary asked.

No Time to Lose

"Well, my dear, you would have managed to do it just as easily if you already had the right technology. Where I come from it already exists." He held up the USB key. "This gadget enables us to, let's say, divert the Internet routes. E-mails are sent to specific addresses in a matter of seconds. With this device I can ensure that the e-mail is delivered at a specific time in the past. Just like you can configure an e-mail to be delivered later, with this you can send them earlier."

"Are you a member of the government?" Stanley asked.

The man laughed. "I'm against the government, and the government that you currently have will be overthrown in a few months." He paused and looked poignantly at each of us in turn. "We offer you three million. One for each of you, if you help to prevent this."

I caught my breath. What to think about such a proposal. Mary narrowed her eyes. Stanley looked at me and then over to the man who had introduced himself as One. "Is that supposed to be a joke?"

The employer did not answer.

"Okay, get out of the car," Stan said.

One reached into his pocket and brought out a few bills. "One thousand for your continued attention."

Stan took the money without hesitation.

Ariana Tiens

"In this time, two young engineers are about to change the world. One of them is going to con the other and strike a deal with some industrialists. Both engineers together have developed a technology that allows for enslaving any person. Even those that possess, from today's point of view, high-tech security won't be safe. With this technology anyone can be located, no matter where the person is, and can be exterminated. It's a powerful weapon that cannot fall into the wrong hands, but will." For a moment he did not continue.

"How do you know all that?" Stan asked.

"Can't you already guess?" One replied and seemed emotionally similar to Mary.

"Are you telling us that you're from the future?" I asked.

"You wouldn't believe me if you didn't already get the small demonstration," he said calmly. "As it stands I don't even have to mention it."

"If you can easily travel back and forth in time," Stan said with a voice dripping with irony, "why don't you travel so far back that you can stop the engineer from even inventing his technology?"

"That's precisely the point. We don't know what the repercussions would be. The man in question is going to make further discoveries that could benefit mankind. We don't know enough about time travel, and even in our time

No Time to Lose

this technology is in its pilot stage. We also don't know when and where the deal is going to happen, and that's what we need you for."

Neither Stan nor Mary said anything. The air in the car resembled a tropical climate by now. I was surprised that the windows didn't fog up.

"I want you to tail the young man and discreetly undo the deal. In return each of you will receive one million. You get everything you need to go underground once the job is done." Again nobody answered. Now the windows really fogged up, and the sky was gray, as if to highlight the gloomy mood.

"I can't claim that it's not dangerous," One continued. "Therefore I'm giving you until tomorrow morning to decide. If you want to take the job, I'll make the necessary technology available to you to minimize the risk. You will close your agency and move to a new office. Then we'll keep in touch until this issue has been resolved."

It felt as if we all were in a trance. This man was deeply unsettling. Ever since he stopped speaking I felt as if I were locked in a dream I could not wake up from. As if connected by magnets, Stan and I turned our heads to look at each other. We communicated with glances. Stan started the engine.

"Should I drop you off somewhere?" he asked without looking at the man on the backseat.

"Drop me off where we started."

***

We drove back to the office and argued half the night. I wanted out. Mary was keen on the job and threatened to quit, if she had to otherwise miss out on the technological gizmos. Stan was drawn back and forth. I knew him by now. He was an adventurer and sought out extreme situations. This was one of the reasons why he had tried to find the author of the e-mail. It was like a spy movie that everyone watched in fascination. Stan wanted to submerge himself in the reality of these movies.

"I can understand that you're afraid," he said after he had asked Mary to give us some privacy for a while.

"Aren't you? This guy has something to hide. Even if this crazy story is true, he's hiding something from us."

"If we have that much money and the opportunity to disappear …"

"That's where it starts!" I said, despairing. "How does he have so much money, and how should we be able to disappear with it?"

Stan took my shoulders into his hands. "Listen, you don't have to come with us. You can stay here and maintain contact with One in case something goes wrong."

No Time to Lose

I closed my eyes. "If anything, I'll be there when you save the world. Otherwise I could never forgive myself."

Stan swallowed and hugged me. "I knew that I could count on you!"

When I went home that night I felt with certainty that our normal lives would be over as of tomorrow. I went through the few rooms in my flat, looked at everything, and said farewell in my mind.

We sat at the office the next morning. The coffee machine ran and bubbled in the background. I had turned it on, even though none of us was thirsty and I was too nervous to drink coffee.

One stood in the door even before our opening hours.

"Well?" he asked when Stan opened the door for him. Stan looked at us and gave us a cocky grin. "Mayne and Partner are reporting for duty."

***

We put up a sign that the agency was closed due to discontinuation of business, and our clients were handed over to colleagues. We were resettled in a warehouse. The lower floor was filled with large items that were covered with tarpaulins.

"If anyone comes by, this is going to look like a disused warehouse or one that will soon be used again," One explained. "Ordinarily nobody deigns to look at this building."

We all watched him eagerly.

"You can go upstairs through this door." He opened a door, and we stumbled into a dark room. Inside was another door. An elevator.

"Wow!" Mary said when we got out upstairs. It was a furnished apartment that housed strange devices. The windows were gigantic. A winding staircase went up.

"I am going to familiarize you with things. And I'm going to explain your job again." One started the conversation. "Upstairs are furnished rooms that you can divide among yourselves. As soon as I have briefed you and we've achieved the first results I'm going to contact you from a distance. Do you have questions before I begin?"

"Where does your name come from?" Mary asked.

"Well, I was the first. The first that joined the resistance and the first that travelled through time. I don't know whether that is going to have consequences. I hope that it has consequences for mankind, if you solve the case, but how long I'm going to live at the end of my journey is uncertain. Everyone only survives one trip back and forth, at least according to our scientists. The technology is, as I've mentioned, not mature enough."

No Time to Lose

He walked over to the devices. "This is a visu-speech. It facilitates communication over long distances and ... space-time. This is how you'll be able to contact me." He pushed a few buttons, and something flickered inside the round machine. As if projected onto a screen the image of a room with a couch appeared in the apartment. "That's how we'll stay in touch." One started when Mary moved to stand beside him and asked how the thing worked. He handed her a thick book. "Detailed explanations for all pieces of equipment," he said.

Mary quickly flicked through the tome. Bedtime reading ...

"You are going to need these." One went to a box that I initially mistook for a computer and pulled out a suit that looked like a wetsuit. A small computer that enabled control was on the sleeves. "It shows possible sources of danger and allows you to circumvent almost any surveillance technology."

The lecture about the suits was long and complex. He had to start over on the next day, because each of us, even Mary, had a swimming head from the new information. The suits could detect body heat, erase fingerprints, and pretty much the only thing they could not do was to grant flight ...

In addition we were equipped with drones that looked like tiny maybugs that were programmed to seek out and destroy plans of the dangerous technology. Once we located the room where the deal was going down, we were to release them, and everything would be taken care of.

We received data and photos of our target person. The young man, named Ben Howard, looked entirely harmless, but his life would go off course within the next weeks. He would create this groundbreaking invention together with his cousin. They originally intended the technology to be used for security and not as a weapon. But combined with another invention, it quickly became a secret weapon ... or rather *would* become.

"If you lose sight of Howard, this could help." One showed us something that looked like night-vision goggles. "With this you can bring up satellite images of buildings that are relevant to your search. All you need are the coordinates. It is best to stand in front of the desired building, if you don't have any data."

"So you can also observe the past from the future?" I asked.

"If you have the required coordinates, then yes. That's why I picked this area, because it cannot be fully monitored at the moment," One replied.

Stan had put on the device in the meantime. One showed him how to set the date.

No Time to Lose

"Hey Mary, did you buy underwear yesterday?" Stan asked. I nudged him in the side.

Mary just shrugged. "No, bikinis. But I have to admit that they look rather similar."

I looked at her in surprise.

"So what?" Mary asked. "We're going to be rich soon, and I need accessories for my private beach."

We received new passports, several of them, with which we could open new bank accounts once we had finished our job. Stan demanded an advance payment, and we bought a new car. We kept young Howard under surveillance and delivered information and images to One. Soon we had the names of possible contact persons.

"I am going to count on it that you will successfully complete your mission," One said solemnly. "The salvation of the world rests in your hands."

Stan declared cockily that it was no problem and that it was only a matter of time. Mary asked whether we were allowed to keep the equipment afterwards, which One confirmed, under the provision that nobody but us could ever see it.

I followed him outside. "One more question?" He stopped and turned to me. "Why are you hiring us, of all people?" I wanted to know, and One briefly avoided my eyes.

Ariana Tiens

"Your names are known in the future. You tried to disrupt the new order. However, you have failed." He paused and looked into my horrified eyes. "You are going to be martyrs one way or another. This way your chances for success are higher, however." With that he left.

Soon thereafter we told One via the visu-speech that we found out when the deal would happen. On that day Stan was the first one out for patrol and began to follow Ben Howard. Mary and I jumped into our cars. I turned the key, and nothing happened. I heard on the in-ear speaker that Mary was on her way to help Stan. "Coleen? Where are you?" I heard Stan ask.

"The damn car won't start!" I said, despairing. My voice was much higher than usual. How could this be? Did someone manipulate it?

"Then stay where you are." The response came from Stan.

"What?!" I could not believe what I heard. I almost screamed.

"The fewer people we are, the less likely we are to draw attention," Stan insisted. "Take care," he said. Then he cut the line.

***

Since then I believed to be powerless: these last hours, until a few minutes ealier and now in this very second. I

No Time to Lose

think I found the solution as the past has caught up with the present. I run downstairs. Mary is about to disappear. "Wait! What if we get Stan out of there?" I ask just as she is about to disappear toward the elevator. "We could travel back in time and prevent that both of you are caught in the first place."

Mary stops and looks back at me unyieldingly. "You heard One. The technology is not mature enough. The long-term repercussions are unknown. Besides, it is uncertain how long we're going to live anyway. I want to enjoy the rest of my life. I like Stan, no question, but it looks bleak for his rescue."

"We have the suits, I still have three drones, we could …"

"We also had the suits before. And don't you think that they have digitally secured the plans by now? Even if we release the drones, what difference does it make? It is too late."

Mary turns around and leaves. I look after her and watch the elevator doors close, making her disappear, then I start to cry. Out of anger. I am angry at Mary, who is too pessimistic, and I am angry at myself, because I surely will not bypass the security systems without her. I try to activate the visu-speech. I have to get ahold of this time-travel technology somehow. Nothing happens. Apparently it is also possible to disrupt space-time communication lines. I collapse.

I don the suit underneath my clothes. I wear a long coat and put the remaining drones into a pocket. I have the location goggles with me. I know from Mary where she and Stan were caught, but the checks were surely tightened. I begin to look for the keys for Mary's car. That should still work, and Mary did not leave by car. I must find Stan. It is the only thing that matters.

"Do you need help?" I twitch and my heart starts to pound when I turn to see Mary standing behind me. She still holds the suitcase in her hand.

"Good grief, child," Mary says coolly. "You want to rescue your Stan out of the gangsters' clutches and don't even realize that someone is taking the elevator in your own home?"

"You are going to help me after all?" I hear myself say.

And suddenly Mary beams at me. "Just admit it, you're lost without me."

I do not know what to say out of sheer relief. But I can also say nothing. Now I know why it is good that Mary never smiles. That face combined with a smile would probably make every man's heart stop.

***

No Time to Lose

Together we drive to the building where the deal went down. I explain to Mary that I assume that the security has been increased. Mary has a laptop and begins to go through the security systems. I sit in the car and turn on the device to look at the entrance during the day. Who enters the building or who leaves. The day is played out in chronological order. At first I cannot believe it. I see it, but my mind refuses to believe what my eyes see.

Three motion trackers, according to the suit's software. The first one is disabled. The others will take a while.

"How do I rewind?" I ask and hand over the device. She takes it, enters the date, and lets it run.

"Have a look," I prompt her. Perhaps I am wrong.

Mary whistles quietly. "That scumbag," I hear her say.

"I think we need to change our plan," I say.

***

We are inside with enabled thermo-cover. That way our body heat is undetectable. Two guards patrol inside the building. Someone lies motionless in a room on the top floor. We split up as discussed. Mary goes to the server room, and I go to the top. Avoiding the guards is perhaps the most challenging part. On the top floor, I do not have to wait long. The lock with the security code is shut down. I enter the room and find Stanley on the ground. He is bound. His expression when he notices me is in between laughing and crying. I remove the tape from his mouth.

"Thank god you are here."

"I'm here with Mary. I wouldn't have made it without her," I say and then get up and release the drones, which spread out in different directions. "Amazing what you can accomplish with technology," I say. "Do you know who was in the building before the deal went down?" I ask and wave with the device that allows us to observe the past.

"Coleen ..." Stan's pupils dilate.

"You know, I thought that we kept no secrets from each other, but that you would betray us—Mary, One, and me—is the worst."

"I kept you out of it," he whispered desperately. "Mary was supposed to get caught. That's why I cut your car's ignition cable. The other party promised to let me go with twice as much money."

Saddened, I shake my head. "You should know one thing, Stan. You don't play me. And this was about more than you and me. It was about the future."

"That's over now. The deal went down. Now cut me loose."

I put the tape back on his mouth. "You know, I also thought that it would be hopeless, but I know Mary. Guess who pocketed USB keys that can send things to the past. I'm

No Time to Lose

giving you a hint—it was one of us. And guess who had the idea to install drone-like programs on all computers in this building before the deal went down. And now you hopefully know who doesn't feel like being jerked around by people like you." I stand up and walk to the door.

"Good luck, Stanley," I say and leave the room.

A Midsummer Night
by Elisa Bonnin

There were a lot of reasons why I would be wandering around disoriented in the Olympic mountains in the middle of the night, a broken sword in my hand and my thoughts spiraling back to old Father Brian, but none that were really very good, or even sane. I kept seeing the old priest as he was in one of the last few lessons I'd had with him, sitting on a bench in my backyard with his white hair and dark skin mottled with age, dressed in that black shirt and pants that all priests seem to own for some reason, his glasses big enough to cover half of his face. He was leaning on his cane, telling me about the nature of our enemies.

"You know, Kayla," he said in that accented English of his, fresh from the streets of Iloilo or Bacolod or wherever it was that Father Brian was from. The old priest was the only person in the world who still called me Kayla. "These things that we fight—they can be evil, yes, but they are not evil in their own minds. They don't care about us. Sometimes they can be helpful, sometimes they do good things. But you have to remember that even the ones who seem friendly, the ones who seem helpful, will not hesitate to kill you. You have to be smart, and you have to be wise, and you have to

A Midsummer Night

understand. Those things are not human. They are not like us."

That conversation was a few months ago, before Father Brian retired and moved to L.A. I was the last student he took on in the Pacific Northwest, the last student since my own brother, Danilo. After what happened to Danny, Father Brian was reluctant to take on any students at all, but I showed a lot of promise and, to listen to the old man tell it, hounded him until he agreed. That sounded about right.

I didn't think I'd needed reminding that nothing I faced out here was to be trusted, but apparently I had. My shoulder ached where I'd been struck, and I finally gave in, sucking in a breath and leaning back against the trunk of a tree. Around me, the Olympic Rainforest continued to hum, trees stretching up to a bright, clear summer night sky. I guessed I should have been glad it wasn't raining. My fingers relaxed on the hilt of my broken sword, a Filipino *dahong-palay*, and I looked up at the sky, taking a moment to catch my breath. My night vision, something I inherited from my grandmother, gave the world a greenish-gold cast, and in the distance the lights of Seattle colored the horizon. I was out here, a sixteen-year-old girl on a Thursday night with no parents or guardians in sight, because I was supposed to be chasing down an *aswang*.

Elisa Bonnin

My parents moved from the Philippines to Seattle before I was born, when Danny was still three. On paper, they moved for better opportunities, but off the record, they moved because of my grandmother. Not because she was sick, but because she was special, something the people out here needed. In older days, they might have called her a *babaylan*, a woman connected to the earth. In later days, they might have called her a witch.

I called her Lola. Grandmother. It was because of her that Danny and I were born special, able to see into the other side of the world. And this was important, because people like us were becoming more necessary now than ever.

In the past, travel was hard, almost impossible. People didn't usually pack up their families and move halfway around the world, and when they did, it happened so slowly that they were usually able to shake off anything they brought with them. That was all different now. People moved all over the world with regularity, bringing their cultures, stories, and memories with them.

And their ghosts. Some places have more than others.

Unfortunately for the rest of the world, Asia has a lot of them. And they are terrifying.

My name is Kase, and I'm a Guardian. Kase comes from Kayla Cristina Cabansag—Filipinos are nothing if not fond of nicknames, and I started life as KC before it got

A Midsummer Night

shortened from there. I started training with Father Brian when I was about ten, a couple of years after Danny's death. At thirteen, I was powerful enough to go out on small hunts under supervision. By the time I was fifteen, I was hunting alone. At sixteen, I was a fully recognized Guardian, with the ability to pick my own battles.

My own *small* battles. I said I was young, not that I was particularly powerful. I was careful not to get in over my head. But this one was an accident.

I was sitting around at home, bored out of my mind from summer vacation, when the agency sent out an alert about a woman who said her cat had been snatched up from the yard by a bird in the dead of night, one that swooped down out of nowhere and made no sound. She described the bird as gray and ghostly with wings like a bat, about the size of a beagle. I quickly classified it as a small *wak-wak* and signed myself up.

A wak-wak is a kind of bird, one with bat wings and razor-sharp talons. On the bigger ones, the wings can get pretty sharp too, but I wasn't too worried about this little guy. They're voracious eaters and eat anything they can haul off, including people. What makes them particularly hard to track down is a trick they play with their sound. They make an infamous wak-wak noise with their wings, and when it sounds loud, that means the bird is far away. When it's soft, that means the bird is right over your head, ready to strike.

The big ones are tough customers and not the sort of thing I'd willingly sign up to go after by myself, but the little ones aren't too bad. I had fought off a couple before and gotten out with minor scratches, so I figured this one would be a piece of cake. I didn't think there was much chance of getting Lady McFluffikins out alive, but the bird's bounty meant a little extra money in the bank, and the action meant that I stopped puttering around the house, driving my family insane. Of course, as you're probably guessing by now, it got a lot more complicated than that.

My first mistake was trusting information from Talim.

Talim was a *diwata*, a sort of elf-slash-spirit, if an elf's ultimate goal was to steal your soul and drag you off to parts unknown. Really pretty, beautiful more than handsome, fair skin and long straight dark hair. Aside from looking like a supermodel that frequently dresses as if he's in a period drama (in clothes from *many* different cultures—Talim thinks of himself as a globetrotter), he would be almost indistinguishable from a human if not for the fact that he doesn't have a philtrum. (Quick, place your finger between the bottom of your nose and your upper lip. Feel that little dip just above the center of your lip? He doesn't have that.)

A Midsummer Night

I had gotten information from Talim in the past, and although he keeps trying to tempt me with food that will make me his prisoner forever, the information has usually been pretty good. So I didn't hesitate this time to drop by his burrow, interrupt his Spanish Renaissance dress-up game, and ask him if he'd seen any freaky bat-birds hauling off helpless kitties around here. After our usual exchange of "No, I really don't want to eat any of your black wormy rice" and "Yes, I'm sure," he directed me to the woods around Lake Quinault.

I had to catch a Gate to get there, ten-mile hikes not being on my agenda for the evening, but after the usual disorientation that came with passing through the elaborate network of tunnels the local Guardians had been building for centuries had faded, I thought I was in pretty good shape. I picked a trail and stuck to it, careful not to offend any local ghosties that might have been hanging around, and started listening for the telltale sound of faraway flapping and impending death.

That was when the ambush happened.

Well, I guess "ambush" might be a bit of a stretch, but it still caught me off guard. I was listening carefully, watching the skies, tracing all the important wards along the trees to let the locals know that I wasn't here to bother them, just an international Guardian trying to track down one of my own, but I still didn't expect it when the bird unfurled its wings and dove from directly overhead, talons poised to dig into my scalp.

Somehow, I managed to move fast enough to avoid the blow, drawing my sword from its sheath and blocking the bird's talons. It closed its claws around the blade of my sword and flapped its wings, knocking me off balance. I lost my footing, tumbling backwards off the trail and down the side of a hill. Broke my sword, tweaked my ankle, landed funny on my shoulder, and now I was helplessly, stupidly lost, wandering around in circles in the middle of nowhere and feeling as if eyes were on me from everywhere.

I fingered the thin slash I had made in the tree trunk a few minutes ago. I was pretty sure I'd passed this particular stretch at least three or four times, and had to fight down a rising wave of panic. To keep calm, I ran my fingers over the belt at my waist, taking inventory of my supplies.

The sword was broken, there was no helping that, but I wasn't completely weaponless. I had my *karambit*, a small curved knife whose handle I could enclose in my fist to make my punches that much deadlier, and my stingray whip, a *buntot pagi* whose sound was supposed to scare away any monsters that came too close. Lola had woven it once upon a time, which was how I knew it was good. Besides my weapons, I had the typical tools of the trade: vials of salt,

A Midsummer Night

ashes, holy water, a crucifix, a rosary, and a small box of tobacco in case I needed to do any *kapre* bribing. Then there were the more exotic implements that living in such an international city necessitated—a stake carved out of the wood of a peach tree in case I ran into anything out of China, *ofuda* from Tsubaki Shrine in case I got ambushed by a *yōkai*, and a good old-fashioned sliver of cold iron in case any of the Fair Folk were around. Aside from the loss of my sword, I was armed to the teeth and I had my training. I just had to trust that I had been trained enough.

I fell back into that training now, going through a mental checklist that I'd prepared for emergencies like this. The first step would probably be to fix the looping problem. In Philippine mythology, finding yourself wandering around in circles in the woods was a pretty common sign that someone or some*thing* was messing with you. Since I didn't think my little birdie friend came with the mental processing power to trap me in an endless loop (instead of just, you know, ripping my face open), that meant I had run into something else, probably a bored kapre having a bit of fun. I sniffed the air for the telltale smell of tobacco and looked around for any hulking, smoking giants, but I didn't see anything. That didn't mean my hunch was wrong, though, so I did what any good Guardian was supposed to do in that situation.

Elisa Bonnin

I took off my shirt. Then I turned it backwards and put it on again. The label chafed at my neck, but a lot of Filipino ghouls had problems with human faces. If my shirt was on backwards, they wouldn't know which way I was going. I picked a random direction and kept going, hoping that that was enough and I wouldn't have to get too creative. It worked. I stepped into a space between three trees with a patch of sky that I hadn't seen before, and only then did I allow myself to breathe and relax.

But not for too long. I was still hunting.

Or, as I was starting to feel was the case, being hunted.

I listened and heard a flapping noise in the air, the steady beat of wings. Loud, very loud. That was good; that meant the wak-wak was far away. My hour-long sojourn into a chain-smoking giant's labyrinth had probably confused it. That bought me a little bit of time. I glanced off to the side, studying my surroundings. Lights flickered in the trees, glittering in the darkness just beyond the boundaries of my night vision. Santelmo, I thought, or more likely just regular will-o'-the-wisps. A problem if I wanted to go chasing after them, not a problem if I wanted to remain right where I was. There was a termite mound that looked like a *duwende* house to me, but again not too big of a deal.

All in all, it looked like a decent spot for a fight. I moved to the side, getting under the trees and muttering

A Midsummer Night

"tabi-tabi po" under my breath just in case any little duwende were hiding out in the grass where I couldn't see them. My sword was pretty much useless now, so I let it fall to the ground, taking up my stingray whip instead. The coils rested heavily in my hand as I crouched in the shadow of the trees, waiting.

I didn't have to wait too long.

I stood behind a tree, listening, as the sound of beating wings grew softer and softer. Then the wak-wak appeared, the little one from earlier that had broken my sword. Its talons were dripping with something wet, making me think that the little kitty cat it had taken earlier definitely wasn't going to be making its way home. I straightened up, stepped out into the clearing to face it.

And then its big brother came charging through the trees towards me.

I didn't think—there was no time. Looking back, I think my heart stopped. I was scared, I'll admit that much. Anyone would be scared when faced with a rampaging demon bird that they weren't expecting. Thankfully, I'd been in enough hairy situations that my first reaction to fear wasn't to freeze up, it was to lash out and *do* something. That saved me. It usually does.

I fished the vial of holy water out of my belt loop and threw it at the bigger creature.

Elisa Bonnin

It exploded on impact, glass shards shattering, sending droplets of water flying everywhere. The wak-wak shrieked and fell to the ground, batting at its face with its wings as it writhed in agony. It was big enough to pick me up and carry me home, so I didn't think that little vial would keep it off me for too long, but it gave me the time I needed to deal with the little guy and maybe enough time to come up with a better plan.

I was in over my head, and I knew it, but thinking about it too much didn't help, so I kept moving.

My whip cracked as I snapped it at the little bird, stopping it from flying right at my face. The sound of the stingray tail at the end of the whip, unearthly loud in the darkness and quiet of the forest, caused it to pull up sharply, wings beating frantically as it tried to reverse its flight. I didn't know what it was about a stingray tail that caused native Filipino cryptids to freak out so much, but at the moment I didn't care. It worked, and I was alive for a few more seconds. That was all that mattered.

I reached for the karambit, its worn leather grip soft in my palm. I closed my fingers around it, the blade protruding from the side of my fist like a claw. At the same moment that the little wak-wak flailed, trying to get away from the snap of the stingray whip, I charged, my hand sweeping past dripping talons to bury the metal blade of the karambit deep

A Midsummer Night

in the bird's chest. I dug my heels into the ground and pulled before the bird could truly struggle, cutting a long gash down the front of it. Then I spun, using my body weight to throw it into a tree for good measure.

Dark blood spattered my hand and the sleeve of my shirt. The karambit was a messy weapon, made for close quarters, and I didn't like to use it unless I was really spoiling for a fight. Still, it wasn't as if I had a choice. I held the claw-shaped blade out in front of me as I turned to face the larger monster, spreading my legs apart and bending my knees so I'd be ready to move if necessary.

It rolled over once on the ground then dug its claws into the earth and launched itself towards me.

I bolted, throwing myself into a patch of moss and soft grass at the side of the clearing. This guy was nothing like the little monster that I'd come out here to fight, the one that I was *prepared* to fight. This one was a real monster, the kind that carried away hikers in the dead of night, terrorized homes in the rural Philippines, and dragged people out of their beds, up into the mountains, where they were never seen again.

This was a witch's hunting bird in some legends, and if I'd been thinking a little more clearly, I might have stopped to wonder who the witch was.

Elisa Bonnin

As it was, I only had space in my mind to worry about the claws, the beak that would eviscerate me if I so much as missed a step, and the wings sharp enough to fell small trees on their own. Father Brian in his prime might have hesitated before going up against a creature like this alone. Lola would probably have done it, but then again, she was one in a million. I was alone, undertrained, and unprepared.

I flicked the stingray tail at the beast, thinking of trying the same tactic, but it didn't work. The way it reared up, barely lifting its head instead of its smaller version's panicked flapping, didn't leave me much room to get in there and start slicing. The holy water had left visible burns on its skin, holes in its bat wings, and gouts of raw flesh across its body, but that only seemed to annoy it, and I was all out of water. This wasn't the sort of ghoul that could be beaten by a little salt and ash, and it couldn't be bribed by tobacco. If I had my sword, the longer reach might have given me a little more confidence, but my karambit was smaller than one of its talons, and I didn't like my chances coming in from the front.

That didn't mean I was willing to roll over and die, though. If you know anything about me, you know I'm not a quitter.

I stood with my back to a tree, bracing myself, and threw myself to the side as soon as the wak-wak came flying.

A Midsummer Night

I let the whip fall to the ground—it was useless now—and launched into a sprint the second I heard its talons driving into the wood with a dull *thunk*. The bird beat its wings, furiously trying to pull its claws out of the trunk, and that gave me the second I needed. I turned, launching myself off of the ground and jumping onto its back, driving my claw-knife into the flesh above its spine as razor-sharp wings sliced through the air around me.

The wak-wak opened its mouth and let out a high-pitched, keening cry, throwing its head back and rearing. I held onto the little claw-knife, determined to keep my grip, but it bucked harder, and I found my fingers slipping. I let go of the knife, and the wak-wak threw me against a tree, so hard that for a moment my vision went dark.

The wak-wak charged at me. My breath caught in my throat, and I fought off the unconsciousness that threatened to claim me, grabbing onto the crucifix hanging from my belt with one hand. The other, I held up as the creature charged, mumbling a Latin prayer, and a wall of light appeared between me and the monster. The bird's claws struck it with a sound like fingernails on a chalkboard. It let out another screech, throwing itself against the barrier, but by then I had already gathered up the strength to move and was hobbling my way into the trees.

Elisa Bonnin

My instincts were right—get away from the open sky, get into tighter quarters to limit its mobility—but the situation was all wrong. I was injured, weak, disoriented, and dizzy, weaponless except for a few half-remembered prayers that—let's be real here—I didn't have the faith to properly invoke. I heard the bird as a rustling sound in the leaves overhead and knew that it was looking for me, that unless I could think of something quickly, my time was up.

That was when I remembered the duwende house.

It was a long shot, a long *stupid* shot, but I was hurting for good ideas, and I wasn't about to let this one go to waste. I looked back at the clearing and saw it there, backlit by the flickering ghost lights I noticed earlier, the fire I could see through gaps in the trees but couldn't name. I gauged the distance between me and the termite mound, took inventory of how much energy I had left in my body, and took a moment to appreciate that if this didn't work, I would probably die screaming and covered in termites. Then I ran.

I darted into the clearing, the open sky above me, and slowed my pace just long enough to make sure the wak-wak was in pursuit. I heard the beat of its wings, whisper soft, and looked up and saw a dark shape blotting out the stars.

And then I put on a last burst of speed, taking cover behind the termite mound.

A Midsummer Night

The wak-wak crashed into the mound, sending dirt flying everywhere, and I felt a sudden wave of power tear through the air. I heard a humming, angry noise and dove out of the way, throwing myself behind a tree and lying flat in the mossy underbrush as I watched the scene.

Lights flashed from the ruined termite mound, angry shrieks rising up from the earth, and the wak-wak thrashed on the ground as the light surrounded it, writhing in pain. There was a crack like a flash of lightning, a smell like ozone rising in the air, and then the wak-wak was gone, nothing more than a dark smear on the ground, and the angry humming of the duwende was all that was left.

Duwende don't like to be disturbed. They're fiercely protective over their homes and bodies and ready to curse anyone that messes with either of those. It's why if you go to the Philippines, you can sometimes hear Filipinos mutter "tabi-tabi po" ("move aside, please") when walking through tall grass, in case any of the little folk are underfoot and listening. I had banked on the fact that the duwende's self-protectiveness and general unfriendliness extended to all manner of life, not just humans, and it looked as if I'd won that bet. I stumbled away from the scene before they could catch on to the fact that I was involved too, mumbled another little prayer to keep myself invisible to any other creatures that might be out there, and stumbled deeper into the woods.

Elisa Bonnin

I didn't realize I was about to collapse until I did, falling forward onto a patch of moss that suddenly seemed like the softest thing in the world. I didn't realize I had been walking in the direction of the ghost lights until I saw one flicker just above me, the last thing I saw before I closed my eyes.

I only intended to rest for a minute, but somehow a minute became an hour, became two, became a length of time that stretched on into infinity. I was aware of a few things while I was out—someone picking me up by the waist, the wind in my hair, a voice whose words I couldn't quite hear, the scent of sandalwood and char. An image, one of the more mysterious ones of the night, of a boy's face. He was standing over me, looking concerned. His features were East Asian—olive skin and almond-shaped eyes—and that wouldn't have been odd if not for the fact that his hair and eyes seemed to be glowing the same shade of red. I remembered reaching for him weakly, my fingers not really obeying the rest of my body as they landed on his cheek.

He felt warm. I thought of fire.

The boy caught my hand and set it gently down at my side. There was blood on his arm, a set of gashes that looked suspiciously like the little wak-wak's talons, but I couldn't be sure.

And then I was out again, like a light.

A Midsummer Night

When I awoke for real, it was because light was starting to spread its way across the sky. I sat up, alarmed, and realized I was alone, propped up against a tree just a few feet away from the Gate that would take me back into Seattle. It was nearly dawn, the sky lightening from the east with the approach of the sun. I patted myself down, but nothing was missing. My clothes were still in place, my shirt still backwards from my encounter with the kapre. The blood had been cleaned off my hands, though, and there was a strip of cloth wound around my left arm, binding a wound I hadn't even noticed I'd had. My whip, karambit, and broken sword all lay in a pile next to me.

On impulse, I checked my phone. This part of the park had a little bit of signal, and I noticed I had about a million missed calls and frantic texts from Mom. I exhaled, still feeling as if I'd been hit by a truck, and tapped out a quick message to her. I was fine, I'd run into some trouble, but I was on my way back and should be home soon. Filial duty done, I leaned back, looked up at the sky, and tried to call the boy's features back into my mind.

It didn't work. Aside from that one image, I had nothing. I felt a momentary warmth settle into my chest and scolded myself for it. Now wasn't the time to be mooning over strange, probably not-human boys in the woods.

Elisa Bonnin

My legs shook and almost didn't want to bear my weight, but I managed to stand up, leaning against the tree behind me as I turned to face the Gate into Seattle. My arms hurt to raise over my head, but I managed to tug my shirt off and put it back on the right way. The Gate would put me out in the I-District, which meant the mother of all awkward bus rides home. I thought about springing for an Uber, or better yet finding somewhere to hole up and call Mom to come down and get me. It was early enough that the Night Market might still be open. If I were lucky, maybe old Mr. Matsuda would offer me a ride. I bent down to pick up my gear, and that was when I heard it. A soft, startled mew.

I straightened up, looking around the woods, my heart pounding.

No freaking way.

Something mewed again, a soft high-pitched sound coming from the hollow where a fallen tree trunk met the ground. I shambled over to it, trying to work some feeling back into my legs, and looked down. A bundle of patterned silk squirmed on the ground, mewling again. I reached out and undid the fabric enough to free the creature.

A calico cat appeared in the tangle of fabric, lying weakly on the bed of silk. There were wet spots of blood in her fur, staining the fabric, but she was alive. I gathered her

A Midsummer Night

up in my arms, silk and all, feeling the bundle squirm as she settled against my chest.

The cat was alive. The thought ran its way through my brain, but I think I was too numb to believe it. I just held the bundle close to me, moving on autopilot as I turned towards the Gate, a patch of air that shimmered oddly and wouldn't have been noticeable if you didn't know where to look. I pressed my free hand to the nearest tree trunk to activate it, and the Gate began to shimmer brighter. Through it I saw the skyline of Seattle, the space needle and waterfront, Mount Rainier looming in the background.

"Alright, kitty," I said, more to myself than to the cat that had found a comfortable spot against my shoulder and waited there, half-conscious. "Let's go home."

I stepped through the Gate, letting the whirl of colors surround me. I told myself I'd leave the mystery of the boy behind, wouldn't think about him again. I reminded myself what Father Brian had said, that these things weren't to be trusted, that they weren't human, that they didn't think like us, but I still couldn't help looking back in the instant before the Gate swallowed us, back at the woods that I had left.

In that last glimpse before we moved forward, through the network of wards and into the city, I thought I saw a red fox watching from behind a tree, ghost lights following it as it turned and scampered away.

Arcane Arts
by Katharina Gerlach

This story is set in the same world as my novel Swordplay and its companion.

Rhianna sat on the chair beside the dark wooden door, her eyes fixed on the white wall beside the window in the corridor, and tried hard to calm her racing heart. This was truly her last chance. What if she bungled it? She wasn't exactly beautiful, and the last fifteen job interviews had taught her the importance of looks. But even if this committee was different and she got the job, what if she failed their expectations?

Breathe in, two, three ... and out, two, three ...

She counted silently. Through the open window she heard birds and the wind, rustling the leaves of the big oak tree in front of Salthaven University's main building. It could all be so peaceful if it weren't for …

The door slammed open, and a tall blonde in a low-cut red dress shot out of the room beyond, floating on a gust of hot air. Her lips were pressed tightly together, and her chest shuddered with suppressed crying. Her long legs,

Arcane Arts

emphasized with red high heels, twitched as if she wanted to kick something. She glared at Rhianna and sailed away.

In her mind, Rhianna compared her mouse-brown braid and her pale skin with the tanned beauty, and her heart fell. If they sent away a sun goddess like her, she'd stand no chance. She'd better leave now and pretend she was sick. Maybe they'd give her a new appointment. That would buy her some more time to improve her looks. Rhianna got up, but before she could flee, a soft voice called from the room.

"Next, please."

The face of a bald, overweight man appeared in front of her. It floated in the air like a balloon, but Rhianna could see the wall through it. She was awed. The simple fact that they hadn't sent a messenger nerl proved that this was a first-rate learning institution. After all, most people disliked the brownish-green, gnarled creatures no matter how much people depended on them. Sweat trickled down her neck despite the corridor's climate-control spell. The semitransparent face examined her from head to toe. Suddenly her no-nonsense dark-blue costume with the white blouse felt inadequate.

"Mrs. Rhianna delSol, I presume? Please, do come in." The face vanished without waiting for a response.

Too late, she thought. If she left now, she'd never get the urgently needed job. She breathed deeply, pushed aside her fear as best she could, put on her poker face, and walked into the room. The soles of her ballerina flats clicked on the floor. The door shut automatically behind her.

The room she had entered wasn't big, but it wasn't small either. The walls were plain white, with a line of pictures of late deans on the left. In the middle stood a desk with four men and a woman seated behind it. Rhianna's throat constricted even more when her gaze fell on the man in the middle, the current dean. The wide, black robe he was wearing couldn't hide his broad shoulders or the way the muscles on his arms moved as he picked up the folder with her application. How on earth could she survive the interview with a man like that asking the questions?

With her mouth as dry as if she'd gone for a long walk in the desert, Rhianna approached a lone chair standing on her side of the table. The sound of her shoes on the honey-colored wooden floorboards reverberated through the room. When she sat down, she felt naked despite her cotton-wool clothes. The dean didn't look up. He kept studying her application and left the talking to the fat man whose projected face had called her in.

"Welcome Mrs. delSol," he said. "What an unusual way to move. I'm assuming you walked on purpose."

His assumption sounded more like a question, so Rhianna felt compelled to answer. After all, people with enough magical control for university had developed many ways of showing off their skills, floating or swimming through the air, or even transporting themselves from room to room. Fixing her gaze on the fat professor, she forced her voice past the lump in her throat with a half-truth. "You know the recommended daily exercise requires three hours of muscle training. Since I am fresh from college and still paying off my loan, I cannot afford a sports studio. Also, I enjoy walking, so I try to combine the fun with the useful."

The man nodded. Rhianna's knees felt so weak that she was glad she was already sitting. Her answer seemed to have satisfied his curiosity, since he pointed with a flat hand at the handsome magician in the middle of the group. "This is Dean Hargrove, the dean. I know it sounds like a joke, but it truly is his name. He's the youngest dean we've ever had."

He introduced the other professors as well, but Rhianna forgot their names the minute he uttered them. Her gaze hardly left the bowed head of the dean. "Dean Squared" stuck in her mind, although she did scold herself for such a mathematical nickname.

The young, clean-shaven man didn't even look up from the papers in his hand. "Well, Mrs. delSol, why do you think you're qualified for the job? Considering your certificate, your marks aren't really what we're looking for. You finished most of your subjects with a twitch or less."

"You are looking for an assistant professor in summoning and thaumaturgical math," Rhianna said, "and I've had clean Laughs in both subjects all through my school years." She marveled at the strength of her voice. It didn't shake one bit, despite the fiery waves rolling through her veins. She sounded as if she were in full control of the situation. "I graduated in those subjects with Félicitations du Jury, and I was granted the teaching certificate for both."

"We noted that." The dean looked at her, and his eyes nearly made her cry. They were the same blue as the sky, but filled with a coldness that froze the marrow in her bones. "However, what will you do if you're called to stand in for one of your colleagues?"

"It's the passion for a subject that defines a good teacher, and I have always loved communicating knowledge. I might be lacking practice, but I am well versed in the theory of most of the other subjects."

She knew she'd lost when the unwavering gaze of his blue eyes pierced her heart. As with every other job interview she'd had, her specialized knowledge wasn't wanted. She allowed herself to relax, trying to ignore the wave of disappointment that threatened to swallow her. There was nothing she could do about the verdict now. Therefore, she decided to enjoy the physical presence of the dean for the short time left during the interview. After all,

Arcane Arts

she'd never met a man this handsome. Plus, he had to be intelligent, too, or he wouldn't be dean.

"Are your summoning skills really noteworthy?" the bald man on the dean's right-hand side asked and smiled at her. "Could you summon something living? Like the pony out there?"

He pointed to a pony in the meadow outside, seeming tiny through the distance. Rhianna shrugged. She knew that transporting living creatures against their will was considered the pinnacle of summoning, but it wasn't a real challenge for her. Getting the horse back to its starting point was the bigger problem. Reverse summoning always led to complications. For her, it was usually a matter of color. Oh well, what did she have to lose?

She blinked, and the horse stood behind her in the room, complete with the grass it had been standing on. Its pungent smell and munching noises filled the room, just like the amazed silence of the professors.

"Surprising," the dean said. "Now take it back. It is ruining our floor."

Rhianna did her best, and the animal vanished in a cloud of rainbow colors. A glance out of the window showed her that the horse's forelock was now bright green. Luckily the professors didn't turn to look, and the spell's remnants would wear off in a few hours.

The bald professor beamed at her. "That was quite surprising."

The only woman—a middle-aged matron of considerable size—bent forward. She wheezed a little when she talked. "I was wondering about your third subject. Can you tell us about it?"

"Arcane arts?" Rhianna's eyes opened wide. This was a question no one had ever asked before.

"Yes." The matron sat up straighter. "What did you learn there? I've never heard more than rumors about it."

"Oh, it's all about nutrition, food, and healthy ingredients," the old professor on the far right said.

"Nerls take care of that, don't they?" the bald man chimed in. "Or if you're talented enough, you simply conjure the food."

The old professor ignored him as if he hadn't spoken. "It used to be part of the curriculum a few generations back. A rather boring subject if you ask me."

Rhianna disagreed, but kept this to herself. After all, she needed the job.

The matron didn't give up so easily. "Why don't you show us a sample of what you learned there?"

Rhianna's heart dropped. She couldn't. Arcane arts were time intensive and required a lot of skill. She couldn't conjure anything like the food she was able to create from thin air. *Wait a moment. I could use the appetizers I made for Dad's birthday.* She smiled and nodded.

"Of course I can," she said, and blinked once more. A tray with small towers of tomato on cheese, cucumber on white bread, egg on paprika, and many more of her dad's favorite kinds of finger food appeared in front of the professors. Five pairs of eyebrows rose simultaneously.

"They look …" The bald man's voice faded away.

"So colorful." The matron reached out and tentatively took a piece of cheese with a tiny tomato stuck on top. She turned it in her fingers but didn't eat it. "This really is impressive. I've never seen food with this much color. And the texture …"

"It really is amazing. It seems you're far better at this than the average nerl." The old professor beamed at her, grabbed a cucumber-on-bread appetizer, and put it in his mouth without hesitating. His smile grew even wider. "This is excellent. Truly." He took another appetizer. "Forget about nerls. This is the real stuff. It seems you're better qualified than we thought you were."

The other teachers watched him with silent amusement as tower after tiny tower vanished. After he'd eaten more than half the appetizers from the tray, the matron seemed to consider it proven that the food wasn't dangerous despite the color, because she finally put the tomato-on-cheese tidbit into her mouth. Her eyes widened with surprise.

"This really is excellent." She grabbed another tomato-on-cheese appetizer. Between the two of them, the old professor and the matron finished off the food in no time.

The dean's smile was grim, but his eyes had thawed a little. "Welcome to the team, Mrs. delSol. I hope you will take care of the food during our annual teacher meeting in June." He held out a hand toward her.

When Rhianna took it, an electrical zing went through her whole body. She could barely believe she would see him again.

***

A few days later, Rhianna ordered a coffee from the nerl-o-mat in the teachers' room while she waited for the dean, daydreaming about a romantic dinner with him. A nerl the size of her middle finger peeked out of the machine. His green face contorted into something that Rhianna knew was meant to be a smile, although it reminded her of a wrinkly child with stomach pain.

"I'm out of coffee beans. Please refill the tank," it said, and withdrew. She picked up the bag with beans and opened the storage compartment, when she noticed two familiar figures outside the window behind the nerl-o-mat. The sun goddess from the day of her interview clung to Dean

Arcane Arts

Hargrove's arm, pressing her impressive chest against his biceps. He smiled and nodded to her, and she fluttered her eyelashes.

Rhianna blinked away some tears. Why was it so hard to bury a dream she knew would never come true?

Dean Hargrove and the woman reached the door to the main building. Rhianna had to bend forward to see them. She wondered why she did. Hadn't it been painful enough to see them flirt? The dean bowed to the woman and breathed a kiss on her hand before vanishing. The beauty gasped and looked around, wide-eyed.

"I am sorry you had to wait," the dean said, his voice coming from directly behind Rhianna.

Rhianna shot round, bumping her forehead on the windowpane. "Sorry, I didn't mean to ..." Her voice faltered.

"There's nothing to be sorry about. The sight is wonderful." The dean gestured toward the window, and she wondered whether he meant the sun goddess, or the softly rolling hills and the city skyline on the other side of the park. He offered her his arm. "Shall we?"

With her heart hammering like a carillon, she took it, and they set out. He showed her around the campus—on foot—and Rhianna did her best to focus on what he said rather than on his looks. His deep voice struck a chord somewhere inside her. She could have listened to him all day. When they neared her lecture hall, the dean said, "You know, I've been trying your walking method for a week now, and found it surprisingly efficient. No wonder gendarmes insist on walking everywhere. It seems my brain gets more freedom that way, and I have more time left for my hobbies since I don't have to go to the gym three hours a day. I have already recommended it to our colleagues."

His smile warmed Rhianna to the core. Was he the kind of man to look past superficial beauty? Part of her heart knew that would be too much to ask for, but another part couldn't stop hoping.

"I'd rather not introduce you to the class. Last term I discovered that an official introduction more often harms a new assistant professor than it helps, but if you insist, I will accompany you."

"There's no need." Rhianna tried to sound confident.

"In that case, good luck with your first lesson." He bowed, kissed her hand, and left.

Rhianna's heart thumped so loudly, she barely noticed the clamor of the students when she entered the auditorium. Her first day as an assistant professor, and she felt as if her legs would buckle any minute. She walked down the stairs past the tiered seating and desks to the lectern and cleared her throat. The noise around her didn't waver, so she amplified her voice magically and began the speech she'd so thoroughly prepared the days before.

"Good morning, ladies and gentlemen. My name is Rhianna delSol, and I'm your new teacher for thaumaturgical math. I will also be teaching summoning in the higher classes."

Instantly the students scuttled to their places and fell silent.

"Now ... I bet most of you aren't the biggest fans of thaumaturgical math, despite the fact that it is the defining force behind many a spell. Since I am new in your class and do not know where you stand, I have prepared a small test." A collective moan went through the students when she summoned the papers and magically distributed them on their desks. "The problems are arranged in increasing levels of difficulty. Work up to the problems that challenge you. If you reach a section that you're unfamiliar with, mark it in green and hand in the paper. There will be no marks on this. It is purely informational for me, so I know where to start."

She heard a sigh of relief here and there. Then, twenty-three heads bowed, and the students began to write. Since the dean had given her a sheet with photographs of her students, Rhianna used the time to make herself acquainted with their names and faces.

Katharina Gerlach

The first three papers floated to her table, and she couldn't help but take a glimpse at them. Only one had made it to the times tables. More papers followed. By the end of the lesson, she knew that ninety percent of her students didn't know how to multiply, and none had ever heard of the Rule of Proportion. A lot of work lay ahead of her. She sighed and summoned her second breakfast: a bottle of spring water and an egg-and-cress sandwich she'd created that morning. Secretly amused, she watched the wide-eyed wonder of the students filing past her who couldn't take their eyes off the colorful sandwich.

In the afternoon, Rhianna determined that she truly had to start at square one with her thaumaturgical math class, or perhaps even at square zero. So she prepared the lessons for most of the term and set to work. Day in, day out, she tried to make the students see the beauty of simple equations and understand the usefulness of balancing numbers. Once in a while she thought she got through, but most of the time it felt like stuffing knowledge into unwilling brains. The only bright moments were when she met the dean in the corridors and he smiled at her. The rest of the days were drudgery. Half of the students in her class ignored her, playing with small spells under their tables, the other half pretended to be listening but were probably daydreaming. Only one girl was actively working, and soon Rhianna found herself talking only to Kate Wilkins. It was gratifying to have at least one student who was really interested in the things she had to say.

One day, close to the end of the lesson, Rhianna noticed Jason nudging Kate. He was one of the good-looking guys, probably on one of the university's sports teams. Reluctantly, Kate raised her hand.

"Yes, Kate?"

"Ehm ... could I ask you a question?"

"You already are, aren't you?" Rhianna smiled.

Kate blushed and turned to Jason. "You can ask your silly question without me." She folded her arms in front of her chest and looked at the ceiling, exaggeratedly haughty.

Jason shrugged and grinned at Rhianna. "I was just wondering what your food tastes like. I mean, it's so extremely colorful. How do you manage to keep the color when you turn, say, a normal tomato into a tomato sandwich? And doesn't keeping the color destroy the flavor?"

"On the contrary," Rhianna said. "The usual way to turn ingredients into dishes steals the food's flavor. I prefer a tomato sandwich where the tomato still tastes like a tomato."

"I could try one of your special foodstuffs." Jason sat up straighter, and there was a gleam in his eyes that she had never seen before. "I could be the guinea pig, if you like."

Rhianna laughed. "I'm here to teach you thaumaturgical math, not arcane arts."

"Arcane arts?" Kate spoke without raising her hand first. "What's that? I've never heard of that subject."

"It's not commonly known. My mother was an arcane arts practitioner. She convinced the dean of my college that the subject needed to be taught, and since I was her daughter, I had to learn about nutrients, flavors, food coloring, healthy eating habits, and more."

"Sounds boring." Jason crossed his arms in front of his chest, but Rhianna noticed that several more students had stopped what they had been doing and were following the discussion. So she considered her answer carefully.

"Tastes great. I'll let you try." She summoned her lunch—a chicken-breast-salad sandwich—and a knife, and cut the sandwich into tiny bits. "Is anyone a vegetarian?" It surprised her that no one was. Maybe the new craze hadn't reached her class yet. When she was finished slicing up the sandwich, she instructed the students to come one by one. "Please take only one piece each, or it won't be enough for everyone."

The students returned to their places. Some had stuffed their piece into their mouths immediately, but others carefully examined theirs before eating. But the bliss on their faces was the same everywhere.

Arcane Arts

"I need to learn this." Jason was still standing beside her desk. "Please. This is much better than thaumaturgical math."

"I'm sorry." Rhianna shook her head.

"Why not?" several students shouted at once.

Rhianna was surprised by the powerful emotions behind their reaction. "For one, arcane arts isn't part of the curriculum. And second, you can't do arcane arts without math."

"We'll do math. We promise." Jason put both hands on her desk and bent forward to better look into her eyes. "If only you convince the dean that we need an arcane arts course."

"Heck," one of the boys in the back, whose name Rhianna always forgot, said, "we'll do math if we could eat this once a week."

Everybody laughed, but Rhianna jumped at the chance. "I'll take you up on that. Prove to me that you're willing to learn thaumaturgical math, and I will create something special for Friday."

"What about a course?" Jason wouldn't budge.

Rhianna thought of the dean's disapproving gaze during her interview. He'd never allow her to teach arcane arts at his university. "I'll ask the dean, but I'm not expecting much. But first you'll need to be able to calculate simple proportional equations."

The rest of the lesson was a mixture of excited whispering and semi-interested questions, but for the first time since she started teaching, Rhianna thought the students were making progress.

***

The class surprised her. For the rest of the week, they worked harder than Rhianna had ever seen them work. By Thursday, even the most untalented of her students had finally understood multiplication. Relieved, she realized that she could get started on the times tables next week. The students most definitely had earned their reward.

So Rhianna spent the better part of Thursday afternoon bent over her arcane arts books. She had shuttered the windows of her arcane arts room to keep out the gazes of curious neighbors. It simply wouldn't do to alert them to the secret lore she had acquired with blood and sweat. Rhianna even moved her nerl-o-mat to the living room. Nerls tended to leach color from the food; some even took the taste.

When darkness fell, she began her preparations. She mixed ingredients, sliced vegetables and fruits, blended liquids, kneaded dough, heated things in pans, and muttered invocations and prayers the way she had learned. She created one delicious marvel after the next, carrying them out of the

Arcane Arts

room as soon as they were done. Muffins, cakes, sandwiches, appetizers, salads—the table in her tiny living room bent under the weight of the food. Exhausted but proud, Rhianna looked at her creations.

Oops! She flinched. *I think I overdid it a bit.* She smiled at herself. With the amount of food she'd made, she could feed an army.

"Silly me," she said to no one in particular. "I forgot the drinks." Chiding herself silently, she put on her coat and hurried out of the house to buy a few bags of apples and oranges. Nothing was better than freshly made juice.

Despite the late hour, she took the shortcut through the park to get to the shop before it closed. The gravel crunching under her feet swallowed the silence around her. Even the cones of light from the decorative lanterns seemed to be drowned out by the night. She'd never seen the park this quiet before, but that suited her fine. She let her thoughts wander as she hurried along the badly lit paths. Her mind filled with anticipation as she imagined the delighted faces of her students. Surely this feast would get them to keep working hard. Maybe the dean would notice if the course's average mark went up significantly. She allowed herself to daydream.

"Money. Now!" Something icy pressed against Rhianna's throat, and her legs froze to the ground. The sting of an immobilization spell burned through her legs, and her scream was swallowed by a muffling spell. "Hurry up, or you're dead."

She tried to trigger one of the emergency-call spells spaced at regular intervals along the park's paths, but the muffling spell prevented her from reaching it.

"Sorry, I don't have any money with me." Her voice simply didn't carry beyond the man's ears, but she kept babbling to gain some time. If she kept him busy, she might find a way to call the Gendarmerie. "I'm a summoner and fetch it when I need it."

"Fetch it, then." The knife pressed closer, and the man's face came into view as he half turned her. He was wearing a mask made of an old knitted sock. There were holes for his eyes and mouth. "But don't do anything stupid."

If the situation weren't so scary, Rhianna would have laughed at how pathetic he looked. Her mind raced. What if she used a reverse summon on him and put him right in the center of a police station? The problem with that was she didn't know where to find a police station. Also, turning him pink or purple or any other color would get her accused of unlawful use of magic, which would allow him to go free to mug another unsuspecting woman.

No, she'd have to think about something that'd render him helpless and make it possible to call for help. She needed more time for a solution. "I will do my best," she said, "but I'm not very good at doing magic under pressure." Most people weren't, so this was a good lie. "Could you take the knife off my throat, please? It would be most inconvenient if I cut myself while trying a spell."

The man glared at her, but took a step to the side. He now held the knife against the left side of her ribs. "Don't dare do anything stupid."

She nodded and blinked. The beautiful cream gateau she'd created earlier that day appeared above the man's head and dropped onto him, heavy silverware plate and all. He screamed in surprise, dropped his knife, and stumbled backwards, spilling the cream all over his head and chest. Rhianna tried to bolt, but the immobilization spell still held. She cursed inwardly. The emergency-call spells! Maybe at least the muffling spell had broken.

"Nine-one-one," she screamed at the top of her lungs. Relieved, she noted that the nearest spell began to flash green. So far, so good. But a glance at the robber told her that she'd better come up with something clever, soon.

Wiping the cream from his eyes, the man bent and picked up his knife. "That was really, really stupid, lady." What little she could see of his face, she knew she wouldn't live long enough for the gendarmes to rescue her.

"I'm sorry. I'm really sorry. I told you I'm not good at summoning under pressure." She summoned a plate of muffins, which landed in her hands. The man lifted the knife and jumped forward, screaming angrily at her. She grabbed a muffin and stuffed it into his mouth.

His scream broke off, and his raised arm sank down as he spluttered and swallowed. He even licked his lips and picked the crumbs from his chest. When his mouth was empty again, he ripped the plate from Rhianna's hands.

"More," he demanded.

Rhianna summoned a plate with cookies and a second one with appetizers. The man ate as if he'd been close to starving.

"More," he said every time she'd summoned something new. He was halfway through a plate with sandwiches when two gendarmes finally arrived. He didn't struggle when they dragged him away from her and dismantled his spells. But when they took the uneaten sandwiches from him, he fought like mad.

"They're mine. She got them for me. Take your fingers off them." He lunged for the plate with the last two sandwiches, knocking over the gendarme who held the plate. The sandwiches sailed through the air toward Rhianna. Before the second gendarme could aim a tranquilizing spell at the robber, Rhianna caught the sandwiches and pressed them into the robber's manacled hands. Immediately, he sank to the ground and took a big bite.

"Wow, what did you put into those sandwiches, ma'am?" The first gendarme got to his feet and took the arm of the robber, who stood up and followed him, peaceful as a lamb, munching his sandwiches.

"Nothing, really."

"Sorry, but we can't believe that. He's acting like a drug addict." The second officer laid a hand on her shoulder. "You'll have to come to the station with us, ma'am." He patted a brown box with the golden markings of a potent spell attached to his shoulder and said, "Team fourteen-slash-five here. We need a drug dog and an invest team on the scene in three."

"Roger," the spell on his shoulder answered.

"I need to go to the shop before it closes." Rhianna knew her protest was futile, but it felt right to at least try. The officer didn't answer.

Three minutes later, a team in white plastic coats arrived, and another gendarme came with a dachshund on a leash. The plastic-wearing men set small black gadgets on the ground around the empty plates and the crumbs and leftovers lying in the grass and activated a spell that created a net of green glowing lines over the crime scene. After that, they allowed the dog to sniff around. Rhianna was surprised to see that nothing moved, even when the dog tried to take a bite of one of the muffins.

"It seems the dog can't find anything," said the gendarme who still held her arm. "Still, we've got to take you in for testing." He led her toward the park's exit.

Rhianna sighed inwardly, but gathered her courage nonetheless. It didn't hurt to ask. "Would you mind stopping at the shop on the way to the station? I need apples and oranges for my students tomorrow."

***

After spending half the night at the station, being interrogated and tested for drugs—negatively, of course—Rhianna managed to gain her freedom at three in the morning after she'd summoned another plate of muffins, this time for the gendarmes. Only when they'd eaten did they understand why the robber wouldn't share.

On the way back, the gendarme accompanying her made a point of going past an all-night shop so she could buy the fruits she needed. Bone-tired, she arrived home, but sleep was out of the question. With tears in her eyes she looked at the half-empty table. All that work, wasted on a gluttonous robber and some suspicious gendarmes. Well, there was still enough to give her students a taste of what arcane arts could be. With fervor, she washed the fruit and fetched bottles before she concentrated on creating the best juice she was capable of with half her mind already asleep.

***

She arrived late at school. At the gate, she passed the blond beauty arguing with the concierge.

"It's an order from the dean." The man grabbed the woman's arm. "You've overstayed your welcome—his words, not mine."

"Ignorant fool. He loves me." The woman tried to push past him, but he stood like a rock in the breakwater. "When I'm Mrs. Hargrove you'll be lucky to get a job in wastewater disposal. Step aside!"

"I have my orders." He put his free hand on her shoulder and turned her with an experienced move. "Please do not come back." He pushed her away from the gate and nodded to Rhianna. Smiling, he gave her enough room to slip through the main gate.

He sent her away! Rhianna couldn't believe it. *That woman was exceptionally beautiful, and Dean Dean sent her away.* With her head lowered and the folder with her notes pressed against her chest, she hurried through the empty corridors, hoping that no one would see her and that her students were behaving. If she made it to her classroom without being seen, she'd stay in the dean's good books. *And with the sun goddess out of the way, who knows what might happen?* When she turned the last corner, she glanced back because she thought she'd heard footsteps, but the corridor behind her was quiet.

Her face and arms connected with a soft wall smelling of straw and wind and horses. As she stumbled backward, two strong arms caught her and kept her from falling.

"Careful." The dean's voice froze her to the marrow despite its friendliness. She couldn't lose the job, not now when it had finally begun being fun. Her mouth opened and closed, but not a sound escaped. The dean smiled at her. "I see that the Gendarmerie had the sense to let you go in time for your first lesson."

The Gendarmerie? How did he know about that?

"I've heard you worked miracles on the students," he continued. Rhianna searched for words frantically as the dean took her arm and led her toward her classroom. "Madame Rubinet said that some of your students actually knew their times tables, which helped enormously in divination. She spoke the highest praises."

"So you've come to see if it's true?" To her, her voice sounded flat, but the dean obviously didn't notice.

"Not really. I trust Madame Rubinet's judgment." He grinned down at her and reached for the doorknob. Only now did Rhianna realize he was wearing riding gear instead of the formal robe of his office. "I came to see how you bribed

Arcane Arts

them into learning, especially since the gendarme who interrogated me had the most interesting story to tell."

Heat shot into Rhianna's face. Without a comment he opened the door and bowed politely. Swallowing her embarrassment, she walked into the classroom, relieved that she had at least been cleared of the drug suspicion. At her lectern, she looked into twenty-three expectant faces that turned as one when the dean followed her into the room. Rhianna thought she'd seen a shadow of disappointment cross Jason's face for a fleeting second.

"Pay no heed to me," the dean said, and walked up the stairs to the back of the room. "I just came to watch."

Rhianna felt her knees grow wobbly again. Being watched by the most handsome man in the school was worse than sitting naked in front of three professors trying to explain the difference between thaumaturgical math and applied thaumaturgical math. To be able to focus on her subject, she concentrated on Kate as she addressed the whole class.

"I am very proud of your progress," she said. "Therefore, I have prepared what I promised."

"You promised to ask if you can teach us," Jason said, without asking for permission first. He turned to the dean. "Has she asked for a course in arcane arts yet?"

Katharina Gerlach

Rhianna wished for a hole in the ground that would open and swallow her. Instead, she went for diversion. She blinked and summoned the first few plates and bottles. A cheer went through the class, and Jason shot round without waiting for the dean's answer. Rhianna blinked again and again until all the food that hadn't been eaten by the gluttonous robber and the juice she'd prepared after her ordeal stood on her desk. She fetched a pile of plates and forks before she announced, "Your reward is ready. Please line up, and don't take more than two pieces at a time."

"Can we go more than once?" Kate asked.

Rhianna nodded and watched her students line up. Her heart nearly stopped when the dean walked to the end of the line and waited for his turn. Why was he here? What would happen if he ate the food she'd prepared? Would he know what she'd done to create it? Her throat grew dry. What if he didn't like it? What if he thought bribing the students was a bad idea? She knew so little about him and his way of seeing the world. Jason stuffed the two muffins he'd chosen into his mouth, chewing wildly, and returned right to the end of the line again. Rhianna watched, unable to move or comment. All she could do was wait, frozen in place like a scared rabbit.

The dean took an egg-cress sandwich, a strawberry muffin, and a glass of apple juice. Rhianna's gaze clung to him as he found himself an empty desk and sat down. Jason stepped beside her. His mouth was already full again, and crumbs flew against her cheek as he whispered, "It was a clever idea to get him to try the food. I bet he'll agree to anything right after."

Without waiting for an answer, he joined the line again that had begun to re-form. Rhianna doubted the dean would even listen to her request, let alone spend the huge amount of money needed to fit a classroom with the necessary equipment.

Her gaze clung to his face as he picked up the sandwich and lifted it to his mouth. She held her breath. His eyebrows shot up, and he chewed slowly and thoroughly. Then he took a bite of the muffin and a sip of the juice. When he licked his lips and dove into his food, Rhianna exhaled and allowed herself to crumble onto her chair. Her knees were too weak to carry her any longer.

For the remainder of the lesson she watched her students and the dean clear off all the plates and empty all the jugs.

"By Jove, that was the best food I've had in my entire life." The dean folded his hands over his stomach and leaned back in his seat. "How did you get it so ... so ..."

"Delicious," Jasper suggested, and other students fell in.

"Tasty."

"Good."

"Delectable."

"Yummy."

"Scrumptious," the dean said. "When I conjure my food, it always tastes a little boring, no matter how elaborate the recipe I'm using. So how did you do it?"

"Arcane arts!" the whole class shouted in unison.

And Jason added, "We need that subject, Dean Squared. You must allow her to teach a course."

"Course, course, course, course," the whole class chanted, drowning out Rhianna's protest about Jason's use of the dean's nickname.

The dean lifted his hand, and immediately the class fell silent. He cocked his head. "Jason Brewster, if you use that name again, you won't be part of any course for a long time, understood?"

Jason blushed, nodded, and sat down. "But will we get the course?" After a short moment of hesitation he added, "Sir."

The dean turned to Rhianna. "What would you need for that kind of course?"

"A fireplace with a cauldron for every student, a wide range of pots and pans, a frost-o-nerl, a fungi-proof storing cupboard filled with herbs, salt, fruit, and vegetables, and a moderate amount of money to buy ingredients."

Arcane Arts

"Are your creations likely to explode when a student makes a mistake?"

"The worst outcome will be a burned pot." Rhianna wondered how she was still able to answer. Her heart raced and hammered as if she'd run a marathon.

"Let me see how much that would cost …" The dean's eyes narrowed in concentration as he calculated, and twenty-four pair of eyes stared at him. No one dared to speak.

Again, Rhianna held her breath, waiting for the answer. A tiny part of her brain registered that she wasn't the only one, and another tiny part kept whispering how handsome the dean looked, but most of her concentration was focused on the dean.

"I think that our budget should cover this, but …"

The rest of his words drowned in the students' cheering. A ball of fire ignited in Rhianna's heart when she caught his gaze. The blue had deepened to that of a warm summer day, and his smile seemed to make her bones dissolve. Gladly, she allowed Jason to pull her into a whirlwind of congratulations and questions. When the students finally left, she was surprised to see the dean still sitting in his place. He got up and walked to the front, where he took both of her hands into his.

"I marvel at your skill in an art not practiced by many," he said, "but I am even more impressed that you kept your wits together when the robber tried to harm you last night. I'd invite you out for dinner if I could find a place that served better food than yours. As it is, all I can ask for is your understanding. Would you go on a picnic with me? I'll bring the blanket and dishes if you bring the food."

Rhianna's heart fluttered, and her soul began to trill a low melody of hope. Maybe the way to a man's heart was through his stomach after all, as her mother had insisted.

"I'd love to come." Her voice was barely more than a whisper, and a scratchy one at that, but Dean had heard.

A smile spread over his face. "But I'll send the dishes back to where they belong. Although I admit that the pony's color faded quite fast."

Laughing, they stood in the classroom until the older students trickled in for their summoning class. As Rhianna watched Dean go, she wondered if he had realized that not a drop of magic was used in arcane arts. Well, if he didn't suspect, he'd soon find out. She turned to the class with a wide smile.

The End

Prophet Motive
by Edd Vick

Aliens shadowed Paul Rohrbach from birth. He was the three-million-and-seventh prophet of the universe, so they must interpret his every act, his every utterance. Each choice he made was parsed and debated to death. Loudly. It made dating difficult.

"He chose Davis Parkway," said the first disembodied voice in his head.

"Collins Street would have been faster," said the second.

"He's used to Davis; it's how he gets to school."

"Still, it doesn't bode well for the Artrins in forty years," put in a third.

"Forty-two years," said somebody else.

That started an argument that lasted most of the way to Luz's house. Not that the aliens didn't comment on whether he'd get out and walk to her door or just honk, maybe even text her phone. Most of the time he liked to do weird stuff, just to see how his observers would interpret their meanings. But today was his first real date with Luz. He wanted the evening to be normal, or as normal as it ever got with nosy, nattering aliens dogging his every move.

Edd Vick

He walked up, slipping a bit on the ice, and rang the doorbell.

"He didn't knock."

"He usually doesn't knock if there's a bell."

"But he could have. That proves the Niskerian Hypothesis."

"Niskeria be damned! It *proves* the Last Among Unequals of the Delta Middilans will be assassinated!"

"Small potatoes."

Some of the aliens had assimilated Earth culture a little *too* well.

Luz herself answered the door, already in her coat and earflapped hat. "Hello, Paul. Hello, aliens," she said.

"Hello, Luz," they all said. Everybody within twenty feet or so heard his aliens in their heads, too.

They'd have gotten away without meeting her father if the aliens hadn't been quarreling so "loudly." The Niskerian faction was in full mental cry as Mr. Santiago clomped down the stairs in slacks, undershirt, and Kermit the Frog slippers. He took one look at Paul and stepped in front of his daughter.

"You didn't say your date was with this *perdedor*," he growled. Everybody in Lashton knew Paul. He and his chorus had been on plenty of talk shows—until it sank in that the aliens didn't talk out loud, just in peoples' heads.

Prophet Motive

"He's not a loser," said Luz. "He's actually—"

One of the aliens broke in. "You just can't equate a simple little murder with proof of a new galactic constant! This could lead to faster-than-light travel! For bodies!"

"Hush," said another. "Hushhush. I want to see how he talks his way out of this one."

"I'll second that," said Luz's father, glowering.

"Good evening, Mr. Santiago. She's safe with me," said Paul. His breath misted in the cold. "Everybody knows who I am. I couldn't get away with jack."

"He's right," said the voice Paul called Mr. Miserable. "Why, the masturbation incident alone—"

"So anyway," Paul cut in loudly. "We're just going to grab some pizza and then go dancing." He shot a desperate glance at Luz, who was bending to look through the gap between her father's bent elbow and his belly. She waggled her eyebrows the way that always made Paul laugh. He bit his cheek.

Scowling down at him, Santiago said, "I saw that reality show they put on about you. Didn't last long, did it?" The show had used a barbershop quartet who parroted the aliens, but their program had been scheduled opposite *White House Brats*. No contest.

"I like Luz," Paul said. "And she likes—seems to like me."

Edd Vick

"He's okay, Papi," she said. "We eat lunch together sometimes. And his aliens are funny."

"Funny!" This from one of the more common voices, one that Paul privately called The Grinch. "The future of the universe is hardly a laughing matter."

"Not that there will be anyone left to laugh in the long run," added Mr. Miserable.

Luz's father gave Paul one of those "you poor bastard" looks, then said, "All right, *mi querida*, be home by midnight, and make sure you take your cell phone."

She waggled it at him as she walked past. Paul followed. She stopped at his car and looked around.

"Where's your entourage?" she asked.

"My what?"

"Those spooks and scientists who always follow you around. That one Secret Service guy who leers at me in English class every day."

It was a wonder he even got to attend ordinary school. For a couple of years he'd been confined to a bunker, being studied, almost dissected, but the ACLU had taken his case all the way to the Supreme Court.

"I asked for a day off," he said. Actually, he had begged, whined, and pleaded, and even so, he was wearing an ankle bracelet. He'd lay odds there was a satellite specially tasked to watch him, and unmarked vans around at least two corners.

Paul started the Honda. He could feel Luz's eyes on him as he pulled into the street. "They're there all the time?" she asked.

"The spooks or the aliens? Yeah, twenty-four seven for both."

"In class, I've heard the aliens talk about what you're doing, and what you're saying. Do they know what you're thinking, too?"

He paused, remembering some times he'd foxed them. "Not really," he said finally.

"I wonder if you're more of a religious icon or an experiment to them." The look she gave him reminded Paul that she was acing science.

Another pause, much longer than the ones that usually fell between comments from his observers. It was as if they were holding their breath. "Where are you going with this?" he finally asked.

"To Satan Claus," she said, suddenly cheerful. "And then dancing!"

"He'll drive there on Warbler Way," said a voice. "If he does, it'll mean the end of fourteen endangered species on Oundle Seven."

Paul chose Fountain Boulevard.

Edd Vick

***

Satan Claus was a treasured relic of bygone Lashton, a pizza place opened by a Scandinavian dyslexic who decorated the restaurant in Christmas colors. Red and green strobes flashed in the windows, attracting moths and downing epileptics for miles around. Inside, gold-and-emerald paper Viking ships covered with dust hung from the ceiling. The funk of decades of grease and onions hung just below the ships.

Luz led the way to a booth near the back. Paul slid into the bench across from her. "He's facing east," said the new voice. "What does it mean? Is that significant?" Paul decided to call this one "Eager Young Space Cadet."

"He's facing her, is what he's doing. She chose this spot, and he's much too shy to sit next to her."

"Still, it's a choice. I think the Vo are going to have themselves a nuclear war."

Another alien said something, but it was in his—or her, or its—own language.

A few heads turned, but most of the diners were students from Paul's school, well used to his celestial chorus. He and Luz were soon ignored again. Ignored, that is, except for however many aliens were currently scrutinizing him.

Menus, water, and service later, Luz transferred a slice of bacon-and-mushroom pizza to her plate then listened as several voices all continued to dispute the impact of their choice of toppings. The minority were contending that something called "the Wuc" would sleep for a dozen more years, while the rest said that the first group's heads were full of dark matter and that Chisnable was going to be the next wave in mind-music. "Do they ever all agree?" asked Luz.

"A few times a year." Paul took a sip of Coke. The glass clattered against the table before he had it safely down. Other people went on first dates and talked about school or television shows or sex. "They get really excited when they do. It's been a few months since the last time."

"Do any of the prophecies mention us? The Earth?"

"Uh, no. Not yet anyway. They're from different planets, all of them really far away. I think a lot of the stuff they figure out doesn't even happen on any of their own planets."

"We mindtravel," said Eager Young Space Cadet. "We cast our perceptions to the skies and explore."

"What made you pick Paul?" asked Luz. "How do you verify his predictions?"

"He was foretold by the last prophet, who may I say was much more accurate. That's how it goes."

"Hey," said another. "Don't talk to her. You know we're not supposed to—" The voice cut out, as if some switch had been thrown. This happened sometimes when they got too chatty about their own goals and methods.

"I think," said Paul, "that for now they're not watching." He realized that a barely felt constant background buzz was missing. "In fact, I know they aren't."

"'We're not supposed to—'" she repeated. "Supposed to what? Reveal too much to their subject, I guess. Or maybe to other people around you?"

"They say it's what I do and say that predicts what's going to happen. Usually they wait 'til after I do something to comment on it. I always thought that if they interfered it would mess up the prophecies, but lately I'm not so sure. After all, I'd never have been on TV or done plenty of other things if they weren't around. Some of what they said today makes me wonder if they're trying to manipulate me."

"Like that bit in the car about which street you'd take. Just today? What's different about today?"

"You." The word slipped out a little faster than he'd meant.

Luz blinked. "Huh. Is it because they think I'd make your decisions for you? No, it can't be that; I'm sure they'd have a huge problem with your parents and school if that were the case. Maybe there's a big decision point ahead of you." Smiling a secret little smile, she nibbled at her slice of pizza then put it down. "Listen, do you like them? Do you want them watching you the rest of your life?"

He shook his head, suddenly hopeful. Whenever anybody had talked about the aliens before, it had been about learning from them or communicating with them or using them in some way. Luz sounded as if she wanted to help rid him of them.

"Good," she said. "Because I sure don't."

What was *that* supposed to mean? Was she just being helpful, or was this something more? Not for the first time, Paul wished he had the cheat code for high school. B, A, B, A, Up, Down, B, A, Left, Right, B, A, and suddenly he'd sail through whatever weirdness lay ahead.

The buzz returned. Something in his expression must have tipped Luz off, because she said, "They're back?"

Nodding, he stuffed the last bit of crust in his mouth. "Done? Okay, let's go dance."

***

Luz insisted on splitting the check. Paul, who was used to a lifetime of exhaustive analysis of his every move, wondered if it was normal for him to question if this was a good thing, a bad thing, or just a normal thing.

***

"If he makes it through this traffic light, the Welterki of the Fiery Snow will finally develop medicine."

Paul hit the brakes.

"Poor, poor Welterki," said Mr. Miserable.

"You *are* trying to manipulate me," he said. Then he added "Sorry" to Luz, who had both hands on the Honda's dashboard and was glaring at him.

She sat back. "*Por su puesto.* I understand."

"Well?" Paul said, not to her. "Why try to control me all of a sudden?"

"It's heretical," said one voice.

"Because we can," said another.

"For your own good," said a third.

Mr. Miserable chimed in with, "Pay no attention to the aliens behind the curtain. It's all in your head."

"Bull," said Paul. "I am not moving until you give me a real answer."

"Good luck with that," said The Grinch.

Paul and Luz simultaneously sighed. A horn honked behind them, and he stepped on the gas.

***

Arms over their heads, Paul and Luz bounced in the tightly packed crowd on The Phar's dance floor. The beat pounded in their ears. The aliens' voices came through in their heads loud and clear.

"North, east, north, west, spin—"

Prophet Motive

There was a confusion of voices as the aliens tried to interpret each change of direction. This reminded Paul of one of his favorite activities when he was a preteen: running around the house while screaming and flailing to overload the thought-stream. It hadn't really worked; they would just work out the implications no matter how long it took, sometimes keeping him awake at night with their musings. Then they'd decipher his uselessly pulling the covers over his head.

They'd always affected him. How could they not? But why pick today to try *controlling* him? Did they think he was going to live with Luz the rest of his life? If so, did they want him to or want him not to? What the hell did they get out of it, when hardly any of his "prophecies" affected their own cultures? He'd always supposed that they could check his forecasts through their mind network; maybe they just liked to be able to warn or congratulate people, depending on whether his predictions were negative or favorable.

Funny. He'd hardly ever thought about his own situation so much. He usually just lived it. It was kind of like paying attention to his backbone. Luz was already influencing him. Then it struck him.

"Influence!" he yelled.

Luz might or might not have heard him, but she did see that he'd spoken. She led him out a side door. Twenty teenagers smoked there, shivering in what little light spilled into the alley from the streetlamp. Paul's ears still rang from the music.

"What is it?" she asked, rubbing her hands along her forearms. They'd left their coats inside. "Got an idea?"

Paul nodded. "Maybe it's not me they're trying to influence; it's other planets. If they can foretell a disaster somewhere and contact someone there, they could give a warning. Or if they can foretell something good happening to a civilization, they can help them along." He spread his hands. "Influence them."

"And the more successful, grateful civilizations there are, the more scientific breakthroughs or impressive artwork or just true believers there are for your mind-sharers. All of their cultures benefit." She looked up, then back at him, and continued quietly, "Not to mention that's billions of people who might not die."

"When you put it that way, it sounds like I've got a lot of responsibility. I wish I could tell when what I'm doing is the right thing. It sounds like they're doing good."

"They're in the perfect position to take sides." She sighed, her breath a fine fog between them. "They could let one faction know about a disaster but not another. If there's good news, they could make contact and take some of the credit. They can make it look like they're guiding the civilization toward success."

"So, they could be either the nicest guys in the universe, or the most underhanded. And they're using me to do whichever it is they're doing. Thanks a lot."

"You're being awfully quiet."

Paul blinked. "What?"

"Not you." She looked up. "Them."

The response was immediate. "*Venga avercuando eleste dormido.*" The words were run together so much he had trouble telling where one word ended and the next began.

It was Luz's turn to look startled. Paul smiled.

"Some of them talk in their own language at times," he said.

"Really?" She bit her lower lip a moment. Then she returned his smile. "Let's go back for another dance."

***

Most of the drive back to Luz's house was taken up by chattering aliens. They debated the meaning of everything he said or did, loudly and at length. It almost sounded as if they were trying to take up every moment of the drive.

Luz spoke over the clamor. "Do your aliens ever lie to you?"

"Who can tell?" He turned the car's heater down a notch. "Most everything they say is an opinion."

"Yeah, that's what I've been hearing. They never gave us anything, did they? Technology, or what their biology is, anything like that."

"Nothing but grief." Paul tried not to sound too morose.

He pulled up in front of her house. For a moment she sat, turned a little toward him. "Thank you," she said.

He wasn't sure what to do. Kiss her? Or try to, anyway. But what if she didn't want him to? Nobody knew better than Paul did how many ways his actions could be construed. There were days, weeks even, when he tried not to make a single important move or decision.

The moment passed. Luz gave a half smile then pulled the door handle and stepped out. "Be careful driving home," she said.

He watched her walk up the sidewalk, saw a curtain upstairs twitch aside then fall back into place, and by the time he looked back she was inside.

"Is he going to hit the steering wheel? I like when he does that; it always means something big. Let me get my charts."

Paul sat, trying to put off bellowing or crying or banging his head on the window for one second. Two seconds. Three. Then he put the car in gear and drove slowly home. The aliens were silent the whole way. He barely acknowledged the Secret Service agent who waved from the house across the street.

It took Paul some time to get to sleep. He spent what seemed like hours mulling over the evening, trying to replay everything Luz had said and done. It felt as if he were the alien, struggling to figure out what her actions meant.

When he woke up, Luz was lying next to him.

***

"He's awake."

Paul had woken to that statement more mornings than not. What he'd never experienced before was that warmth at his back, that arm thrown across his side. When he turned over, there she was.

"Gah!" he said.

"Good morning," said Luz, yawning. "I was waiting for you to wake up. Your entourage said you usually wake up around six thirty on school days."

Paul froze. He distinctly recalled leaving Luz at her own house last night. While he certainly wasn't unhappy to see her, this wasn't exactly how he'd planned their next meeting.

Luz sat up on the edge of the bed. She was still dressed. "Sorry. I fell asleep."

"What are you doing?" It came out a little more abruptly than he'd wanted. He cleared his throat. "I mean, I didn't expect—"

"That's okay. I just got sleepy there at the end." She stretched. "I was here to test a theory, and because I was invited."

"Invited?"

"Earlier today, when you thought one of the aliens was speaking in his own language, he was actually asking me, in Spanish, to come see you after you were asleep."

"What? Why?"

"So he—or she?—could talk to me while you weren't awake, of course."

Paul grabbed his pants off the floor while she continued. He tried to be quiet so he wouldn't wake his mother. God knows what she'd say if she found Luz in his room.

"Which brings us to what I've pieced together." She turned away as he struggled under the covers to get his pajama bottoms off. "There's a prophecy war brewing."

He waited.

"It was that Welterki prophecy that got me started. Prophecy shouldn't equal causation. If you do or don't do something, then two completely different results—" She scowled. "No, not 'results.' The interpretation if you do something should not just be negated if you don't do it. There should be some other event somewhere completely different. Oh, wait! It's a second-order problem—of course!" She slapped her head. "If they try to influence you, then whether or not you accept is indeterminate, with a forking set of prophecies. I wish I had a whiteboard in here ..."

"But that Welterki crack—"

"Exactly. There are two factions of aliens. The traditionalists are like priests; they just want to interpret your actions like their ancestors have for millennia. And, like I said, profit off of them." She shrugged. "But recently a few newer ones have come along who are more, oh, inquisitive. They're interested in seeing what happens if they 'encourage' you to act in certain ways."

"Why now?" he said, then the light dawned. "Oh." Before Paul, every prophet had been an adult, well set on carrying on their normal lives. Paul was the first one to be determined to act oddly. He looked up. "They're being awfully quiet."

"They want to know how you're going to react," said Luz. "Your gift of prophecy is predicated on your free will to make choices. But short of being severely disabled, you probably have less free will than anybody ever. You're surrounded by Secret Service agents and scientists, not to mention aliens intent on manipulating you now."

Paul stood up to button his shirt. Yesterday, when she'd wondered what was making the aliens act differently, he'd said it was her. He'd been more right than he knew. All they'd talked about was the aliens; he'd thought she could help get rid of them. Now he wondered if she had been sent by some government agency or another, maybe even from some other country. It was obvious she'd been thinking about his situation for a long time.

"They wanted to talk to you when I wasn't awake, and you wanted to talk to them when I was asleep." Slipping bare feet into sneakers, he casually reached for the phone on his bedside table.

"He doesn't trust you," said one of the aliens. "That device conceals a transmitter to agents of the Secret Service."

"Guys!" The moment it slipped out he realized how stupid it sounded. They'd never been his friends; he'd just grown used to them. He looked at Luz.

She didn't move, though she was paler. "Go ahead, if you want," she said quietly. "But I am doing what's right for you. At least I think I am."

He felt a flash of anger. "What's right for me. That's what the aliens said yesterday. 'For your own good.' So you're, what, working with them?"

"You're a pain in the ass, Paul," she said, finally smiling. "You mess with them all the time, by making weird choices, or too many inconsequential ones, or by trying not to make any choices at all. You aren't the first prophet, you know; you're just the latest in a long line of them. Being made into a prophet so young has messed you up big time." She reached out with one finger and almost touched his forearm.

"Some of them said they want to get rid of you, too," she added.

"Some? 'Get rid of—?'"

"Actually, just the priest types. I guess if they startle you at the right moment, you might step in front of a car or drive off a cliff, but that's a last resort. They say they'll find the next prophet a lot easier if you work with them." She frowned. "I'm sure there are ways to improve the process. Evidently prophets are just people who are better tuned in to how the universe is trending, and that helps each one foretell the next." She checked her watch. "Ready?"

"Ready? To foretell my successor?"

"For breakfast. I told your mom we'd be down by seven."

"You ... told my mom?"

"Well, sure, but all I told her was that we were going to have sex, nothing about talking to the aliens."

***

His mother was surprisingly happy that Luz was joining him for breakfast. She served them bacon, toast, and eggs, with orange juice. It was a thoroughly normal meal, not like many he'd demanded in the past. He refrained from singing, from insisting on chopsticks, from marching around the table leading an invisible band.

"That was a bite of toast, two of egg, then a sip of juice. The Kanjarians are going to discover a comet heading for their moon colony and successfully divert it."

"Agreed? I mean, yes, agreed," said another voice.

Eager Young Space Cadet chimed in. "That … sounds right."

Luz paused with a bit of egg on her fork. "Nice work; you're getting them to agree."

Mr. Miserable said, "Pfft, hardly. It means the Minnidee are about to enter a new dark age."

Luz grimaced.

Paul slammed his glass down, sloshing juice over half the table. "Why can't they just leave me alone!"

There was a babble of voices as each alien tried to decipher his outburst. This, and the crestfallen look on Luz's face, finally convinced him they were not colluding to trick him in some way.

He grabbed a rag and began to mop up the spill. "How do I fix this? What do I do?"

"Go through a normal day for once," said Luz. "Do just exactly what a normal high schooler would do. Don't make weird choices, or too many or too few of them. Just be what you would have been if they hadn't come along."

Prophet Motive

"I'm not sure I know how."

"You were pretty normal with me last night. Maybe we could go through the rest of the day together."

None of the aliens spoke, but the buzz in his head intensified. It was as if they were all holding their breath, whichever ones of them breathed.

"Okay," he said, feeling oddly light-headed.

***

Paul screwed it up. How could he not? Normal was as alien to him as his voices. When the aliens distracted him from catching a pass during football practice he screamed at them for three minutes straight. His teammates took it in stride, but it sent the voices into a several-hour argument.

He spoiled the next day, too, and the one after that, but each became easier with Luz's help. She made lists of normal activities, she met him between classes, and she got him involved in a perfectly ordinary snowball fight. She distracted him from the aliens, the government agents, and the documentary crew that suddenly showed up.

She kissed him in a perfectly ordinary way that to him felt utterly unique.

The next Friday evening came at last. All day his aliens had been largely in sync. Even Mr. Miserable made fewer dissenting predictions. Luz agreed to go out with him again.

***

Edd Vick

Satan Claus looked, sounded, and smelled the same as always. Paul grimaced at all three, but it had seemed like the natural place to go.

"Your dad didn't seem as upset to see me this time," he said.

She looked down and played with her hair. She'd braided it tonight. "I had a talk with him. I said you and I would probably be seeing each other pretty often."

Paul grinned. "I'd like that." He barely listened as his backing group conferred over his statement.

"There is one thing, though." She looked up again. "I'm applying to MIT, and I want to know if you've made a decision about college yet."

Some part of Paul panicked. Panicked because he wasn't ready for any question of this magnitude. Panicked because the day had been going so well. Panicked because he wanted to say sure, he was going to Boston, too, and at the same time wanted to say he was going anywhere *but* there. If the aliens accompanied him to a new city, a large one, his life would be a whole new hell. The decreasingly rational part of his brain knew he was going to have to say something soon.

"I don't know," he said, reaching to take her hand. "It's ... too early to say. But I think I'd like to talk it over with you some more. A lot more."

Prophet Motive

Her hand moved, her fingers shifting to intertwine with his.

"*YOW!*" The mental shout was so loud that people dropped forks, glasses, and slices of pizza all around the restaurant. Luz and Paul jerked apart.

"It's the next prophet!"

"It is! I can see where she is."

Mr. Miserable said, "I'm certain she'll be just delighted."

Paul ignored the angry stares, scarcely daring to breathe. "That's it? If they found the next prophet they—they're really going to go?"

"It looks so," Lux said. "I did help them refine the procedure for narrowing down the possible locations based on where earlier ones were."

A horrible notion popped into Paul's head. "*You* aren't the next prophet, are you?"

"Oh God no." She waggled her eyebrows at him. "She's three thousand light years away."

"Three thousand and fourteen," said The Grinch.

"There. See?"

"Boston?" he said, reaching for her hand. "I'm not sure my grades are good enough, but I think I'd like to try."

Edd Vick

The aliens stayed with them through dinner and dancing, making their usual pronouncements in multi-part harmony. Paul drove Luz home and parked.

"It's time to say good-bye to Paul," said The Grinch. One by one the voices came to say their farewells, each one fading out at the end of their sentences. The last one to leave was Mr. Miserable.

"Take care of yourself, Paul. Try not to screw up too much. We'll be seeing you." His voice grew fainter then disappeared, taking with it the buzz in his head.

Paul straightened up in his seat, looking out the windshield at a perfectly ordinary midnight. Finally he could relax.

Then he frowned. "Be seeing you?"

Luz, uncharacteristically, giggled. Just a little, as if something had tickled her in an unexpected place.

The buzz returned.

"Hello, Luz," said Eager Young Space Cadet. "Ready to take notes on the next prophet?"

Paul bit his lower lip. "You're—? Don't tell me you're going thousands of light years away?"

"Of course not, silly," she said. "My body will be right here. I'll just be another voice in the new prophet's head."

The End

Robyn's Gift
by A. M. Kremer

The sun was just rising, painting the horizon pink and gold and orange. In the village, everything was still quiet, devoid of the busy industry of daytime. The cool morning air already held a hint of the heat the day would bring, of burning sun, dazzlingly bright, and possibly a violent thunderstorm later. But for now, the morning was cool and pleasant, with just the slightest bit of tension in the air.

Standing on the highest tower of his father's castle, his arms resting on the crenellations in a pose that was both comfortable and possessive, Robyn took it all in, savoring the sights and the fresh air and the quietness. For the first time this week, he really felt like the lord of the manor, felt that the lands he overlooked were really his.

Well, technically, of course, they weren't. But his father had left on the king's orders a week ago, going on a military campaign, for the first time leaving his eldest son in charge instead of his wife or his steward. Robyn had been very proud, and secretly relieved, too. After all, this could be seen as tangible proof that, despite their differences, his father trusted him, thought him capable of such a task. Underneath all that, however, in a dark place that he never let anyone see, he had been a little scared, too. The responsibility had felt like a heavy cloak, weighing down on his shoulders and making it just a little harder to breathe. And much of the time, it still did.

There had been moments when he had felt like a silly little boy playing with his father's sword, pretending to be a great lord, although he had done his best not to let anyone see his insecurity. So far it had gone surprisingly well, although he secretly suspected that half of it was due to everybody helping him, wanting him to succeed while never taking him entirely seriously. It was a disconcerting thought, but one he could never quite shake. Maybe Lyell, his tough, middle-aged arms tutor, veteran of many of the king's wars, was right when he told him to just stop thinking so much. But that was something Robyn had never been able to do.

Now, however, for the first time, he was feeling it. He felt confident, in control, as if everything was as it should be. Being awake when everyone else was still sleeping gave him a strange feeling of possibility, of omnipotence almost, of a solitude that wasn't painful but rather strangely intoxicating. Savoring the feeling, he let his gaze wander over the peaceful landscape below—the village, the glittering river, the forest in the distance.

Robyn's Gift

He imagined himself commanding an army, valiantly defending the castle against an invading force. His heart began to beat a little more quickly as he imagined the thrill of the fight, the chaos of steel and blood and shouted commands, the bright colors of the sun reflecting off armor, defiant banners streaming above. He could almost hear the sounds of combat, could almost see the army approach in the distance, little specks of color from their banners, glittering silver reflections as the rising sun caught polished steel.

Or ... could he? Suddenly, Robyn was alert, leaving his daydream behind in an instant. He had enjoyed imagining himself a valiant battle commander—until he wasn't quite sure anymore that the troops were only there in his imagination. He looked closer, looked until his eyes were burning. It was nothing, he decided, just the sun as it rose above the horizon, playing tricks on him with its colorful light falling in at an odd angle. There were no banners there, no armored enemy knights. Except he still wasn't quite sure.

Down below in the bailey, people were beginning to be about their business. The castle was waking up. Robyn knew he should have gone down to have breakfast and started with his own duties, to show that he was in control. But he couldn't, not yet. First, he had to make sure that the army wasn't actually there. Maybe it was stupid, but otherwise he wouldn't be able to focus on anything. Maybe he was letting his imagination run wild. Maybe he was worrying too much. People kept accusing him of both. His tutor, his father, pretty much everyone who counted. But what if, this time, he was right?

While the sun rose steadily higher in the east, changing color from pink to orange and, finally, to bright yellow, Robyn kept his lookout, straining his eyes, trying to make out the shapes in the distance. He had the feeling that they were moving, coming closer. But that, too, might be an overactive imagination at work. He thought about taking someone up with him, maybe one of the younger squires who were too respectful of his new rank to ask awkward questions. But he couldn't bring himself to do it. What if he was, indeed, imagining things? He would look like a fool or, worse, a madman, dangerously unreliable. Hardly the right way to inspire confidence in the people he had to lead. He knew only too well how rumors spread and steadily grew in the confined space of the castle with its many different inhabitants. The thought of everyone gossiping about the lord's crazy eldest son, scared of his own shadow, was too much to bear.

So he waited. The sun rose steadily high over the horizon, gradually driving away the shadows and morning mist. Robyn could feel its warmth on his bare face and hands, but he registered it only in an offhand, distracted way,

Robyn's Gift

his main focus staying on the horizon. Had that been a movement? Another reflection?

Soon, there was no question anymore. With icy certainty, Robyn realized that what he had seen was, indeed, an approaching army, complete with banners, outriders, and something that might be siege engines following at the back. Suddenly, he realized that an overactive imagination would have been preferable, even if it would have made him feel like a fool. Better that than having an army that he had no idea how to deal with at his doors.

In the moment it took for worried uncertainty to become cold fact, the would-be warlord turned into a frightened boy. Robyn stood frozen, unable to move, terrible scenes playing out in his mind's eye. Why oh why had his father left just now? He knew how strategically important the castle was, knew how likely an attack was in the current political chaos. He had rivals, more than enough of them, some at odds with him for political reasons, others for sheer personal rivalry. How could he have left Robyn alone with this?

He left you alone because he knew you could handle it. Now, don't disappoint him, a quiet voice said in Robyn's mind. It cut through the fear and chaos, sounding authoritative and reasonable. The way he should be. Robyn took a deep breath. This was not the time for frightened boys, and he wasn't one. From this day on, he was a man, a man who had been trained in warfare from early childhood on, who would do whatever it took to keep the castle safe.

***

Night was falling. Robyn felt tired, his limbs heavy with constant exertion and lack of sleep. It was the fifth day of the siege, or maybe the sixth. Robyn had lost track. Time had become meaningless in an endless series of assaults, counterattacks, and merciless volleys by the enemies' trebuchets. But so far, they had beaten back every attack. So far, their defense was holding.

Someone shouted a warning. Robyn turned his head and saw a sentry farther down the wall point down at something Robyn couldn't quite make out. His reaction was pure instinct. With a swift gesture, he grabbed his helmet, which had been lying on the ground, put it on over his mail coif, and slipped on his mailed mittens. "Follow me!" he bellowed, picking up his sword and shield, raising the weapon in a "forward" gesture. He didn't look back. He knew his men would be following him—had to believe it.

In the scarce light of a few flickering torches, Robyn rushed over the battlements. Panting, he reached the section of the wall the guard had indicated. The guard, a veteran member of the castle garrison, was already engaged in a desperate attempt to push something off the wall. Robyn swore softly under his breath.

Robyn's Gift

"Scaling ladders. Don't let them get up," he shouted to his men.

Gripped by the excitement of battle, Robyn felt all tiredness leave his body, his senses sharpening unnaturally. It was a feeling almost of happiness, of wild, uncomplicated joy, although he knew the darker currents lurking just beneath the surface. With a battle cry, he stormed towards the ladder.

It was not a moment too soon, because one of the boldest enemy soldiers, probably eager for glory, had all but reached the wall. When he saw Robyn engage, he made a last desperate effort, gaining the wall, finding his footing, and bringing his shield, which he had been carrying slung on his back so far, into position.

Robyn didn't hesitate. Again screaming his battle cry, he engaged, pushing his opponent backwards with wild, swift strokes. For the briefest moment the man seemed surprised, but he managed to bring his shield up in time, parrying the next blows easily. When Robyn was least expecting it, the soldier counterattacked, made a vicious lunge that glanced off Robyn's shield, burying the blade in Robyn's left shoulder.

Robyn felt no pain, not yet. That, too, was part of the strange battle wildness. The distant realization that he had been hit, however, was enough to bring him to his senses, to become aware that he was wasting his energy with his wild, uncontrolled attacks. He slowed down, just a little, trying to anticipate his opponent's actions. For a short while, they were locked in a deadly dance of attack and counterattack, of cuts, thrusts, and blocks. Neither gained a significant advantage.

Then, however, Robyn felt more than he saw his opponent's stance shift, ever so slightly. When the attack came, the man's sword and shield clashing against Robyn's with the full force of his athletic body behind it, Robyn was prepared. His slighter build was a disadvantage, but he knew what to do. In a dangerous maneuver, he ducked, sidestepped, somehow managing to find sure footing on the narrow wall. His next blow landed behind his opponent's shield, wounding his arm, making him drop his guard.

Robyn wasted no time seizing the advantage. With a scream, he buried his sword in his opponent's chest, never looking away as the older man froze as if in surprise, twitched, then fell down and lay still. With an effort, Robyn pulled out his sword and went to search for other opponents. "Try to push down the ladders. We have to end this," he shouted to his men before throwing himself back into the fray.

***

Robyn's Gift

Robyn couldn't have said how long it took, but finally they had succeeded in beating back the assault. Their opponents, unwilling to suffer any more losses, had withdrawn. For now, it was quiet.

Robyn sat in a corner of the guardroom, having one of the surgeons tend to his shoulder wound. His hauberk and padded gambeson had prevented the worst, but by now he was beginning to feel the pain, as well as the exhaustion after days of little sleep, much fighting, and even more worry and tension. It was like a huge, dark weight closing in on him, almost suffocating him. He wanted desperately to be alone, but of course that was an illusory idea for the person who was, nominally, in charge of everything, of running the castle as well as defending it.

When a shadow fell over him, he looked up wearily, brushing his fair hair out of his eyes with his free right hand. The newcomer was Jonis, his father's steward. Robyn sat up a little straighter, determined to make an effort not to show weakness in front of a man he had always respected for his quiet competence.

"How is your shoulder?" Jonis asked, his voice slightly concerned, but calm and quiet as usual.

"Just a scratch. My armor held off the worst part," Robyn replied, trying to sound more confident than he really felt.

"Good. Make sure to have your hauberk repaired immediately. You'll need it tomorrow," Jonis said, not quite able to let go of the teacher and advisor role.

Robyn just nodded. He didn't even want to think about the next day, the next battle.

Jonis gave him a long, thoughtful look, then said quietly: "Come to my quarters when you're done here, please. I would like to talk to you in private."

***

"Let me speak to you openly," Jonis said when Robyn had sat down opposite him in the privacy of the steward's quarters.

Robyn nodded. Conversations that started like this were hardly ever pleasant, but he was no coward. He would have to deal with whatever it was that Jonis was going to tell him.

"Don't look at me like that. I'm not going to criticize your leadership or fighting skills," Jonis said, a note of warm amusement coloring his voice. "Very much the opposite, in fact. You have been holding up remarkably well during the last few days. I know you have often been at odds with your father, but if he could see you now, I know he would be very proud of you."

Despite everything that was going on, Robyn felt warmth spread inside him, felt his face grow hot and a smile appear on it. "Thank you," he said, trying not to be overwhelmed by unexpected emotion. Jonis was one of his father's closest confidants. If he said something like that, it just had to be true.

Jonis smiled, but after a moment, he became serious again. "However, no matter how well we fight, we won't be able to hold out much longer," he said, his voice harder now.

Robyn opened his mouth, wanted to deny it, to vow that he would hold the walls, somehow. But the desperate pledge died on his lips when he saw the implacable certainty in Jonis's eyes, a quiet knowledge of the inevitable that held no sign of reproach.

"They're just too many, too well-equipped. It has nothing to do with bravery; it's tactics. The reality of battle. And despite your youth, you know it, too. I've seen it in your eyes," Jonis said.

Feeling utterly defeated, Robyn nodded. He didn't trust his voice enough to speak, but Jonis got the message anyway. He eyed Robyn with an expression the younger man couldn't quite decipher, silent for a moment. "There is, of course, one last chance to turn this around," he said after a while. His voice was entirely matter-of-fact now, but there was still this strange expression in his eyes.

Robyn looked at him in confusion, his tired, defeated brain incapable of figuring out what this latest turn in their conversation was about. "What chance? And why didn't you mention this earlier?" he asked, harsher than he had intended, trying to regain some control over the situation.

Jonis took no notice of his tone. "I didn't mention it earlier because I know you won't like it. I wanted to exhaust all other options first. But now, things are desperate, our defenses are crumbling, and I feel I have to bring it up."

Robyn watched him intently, hierarchy and pride quite forgotten. "What is it?" he asked quietly.

"Well, we would have to ... employ nonconventional means of defending ourselves," Jonis answered. "After all, it's an open secret that you have been doing more than just reading old books, all those afternoons shut in your room with that old traveling artist."

A feeling of icy cold engulfed Robyn as he realized what Jonis was suggesting. Suddenly, he recognized the emotion in the steward's eyes. It was pity.

"Just a little bit longer, Mama. Just let me watch some more tricks. Please?" Robyn pleaded, looking up at his mother.

Robyn's Gift

She sighed. "All right, then. But only a few minutes. We must get back to the castle. There's a banquet tonight."

Robyn thanked her, beaming, already turning his attention back to the bearded old man in his colorful tunic.

The spring fair was always a happy occasion, exotic and exciting and full of sights, sounds, tastes, and smells very unlike anything he usually came across. But this year, it was even more special, because this old man was unlike anything, or anyone, he had ever seen. He was showing magic tricks, which in itself wasn't so remarkable. But something about how he did it was different. It wasn't just the way it all seemed a little more elaborate than what the others did, a little subtler. Nor was it just the fact that, try as he might, Robyn never managed to come up with even the slightest idea how the artist did it. No, there was more. Watching the man perform, Robyn felt a strange sensation, as if the air around the old man was filled with energy, shimmering in exotic, ever-changing colors, like hot sun on a summer's day. Robyn couldn't quite describe it, but he was mesmerized. No matter how long he looked, it was never enough. It only deepened the mystery.

For the duration of the fair, Robyn came to watch the old man perform every day. Eventually, of course, the artist took notice of the fair-haired boy in the richly embroidered tunic who never seemed to get enough of watching him.

Finally, on the last day, he addressed him directly. They were quite alone, the other fair-goers looking elsewhere for amusement.

"Are you enjoying my show?" the old man asked. His voice was kind, full of friendly curiosity, and Robyn, although he was normally shy, felt surprisingly at ease.

"Very much, sir," he said honestly.

The old man chuckled. "Don't go calling me 'sir,' young gentleman. I can see that you're high-born," he reproached gently. "We have to play by the rules." Robyn nodded silently, although he wasn't quite sure what the old man meant by the last sentence. "I'm Master Nichasin. But you can call me Nichasin."

"I'm Robyn. My father is—"

"Oh, I think I know who your father is," the old man interrupted. "So let's talk about why you keep coming back here."

Robyn considered it for a moment, and decided that he would try to be as truthful as possible. Somehow, he felt as if Nichasin would see through any lie he told, anyway.

"I don't know, I just ... like it," he said. "It's like something out of a story, out of another world. As if ... as if there is something in the air, a strange power. I can't really describe it." He fell silent, feeling stupid, but Nichasin eyed him with renewed interest.

Robyn's Gift

"Something in the air? Now that's interesting," he said quietly. "Because sometimes, performing fancy tricks is just something you do to hide a much greater truth."

Robyn eyed him quizzically. "Which truth?" he asked.

"Well, young master Robyn," Nichasin said gravely, "do you believe in magic?"

With a start, Robyn came back to the bleak reality of the steward's office and a castle encircled by an enemy army. The memory had been vivid, brought on by Jonis's mentioning of his "special studies." In the years after that first meeting, Nichasin had often come back to visit Robyn, and he would spend time with Robyn talking, going over ancient tomes together, teaching him. Because Robyn, for some reason nobody understood, had an affinity towards magic—or, as Nichasin preferred to call it, "The Arcane Arts."

Robyn's father hadn't been thrilled about these studies, insisting that his son and heir should concentrate on his swordplay and the other skills befitting a future lord of the manor. But Robyn had quietly insisted, thoroughly fascinated by the world Nichasin and his books opened up to him, and his father, perhaps sensing how important the studies were to Robyn, hadn't pushed the matter.

Jonis eyed Robyn, intent, thoughtful. Robyn shifted uncomfortably under the older man's steady gaze. "I can't do that. You know I can't," he said, a rough catch in his voice betraying his emotional turmoil. This was the exact situation Nichasin had warned him about. Robyn remembered it as if it had happened yesterday, although it had to have been years ago.

"But this is ... powerful. With these arts, you could do a whole lot of things," Robyn said. The evening sun was casting a golden glow into his father's solar, where he and Nichasin had retired to study. Nichasin nodded, prompting him to go on. "So, why do you ... why do you just travel around fairs, performing tricks to children and village lads? There is so much more you could achieve. I don't understand."

Nichasin smiled at him, but it was a sad smile that made Robyn feel uneasy. "Well, think about it, young Robyn," he said, his voice kind but quietly intense. "If I used my skills for power, to change the fate of the kingdom, what do you think would happen?"

Robyn thought about it, thought long and hard. "I don't know," he finally admitted.

Nichasin didn't look angry. He was a patient teacher. "Well, if I did it once, I would never have peace and quiet again," he explained. "Everybody would try to get me on their side. Power plays. Intrigue. All those things the lords love. Yes, boy, your father, too, although he is more

Robyn's Gift

honorable about it than most. If people found out what I can really do, there would be no security, no peace. If I changed the fate of the kingdom once, it would forever be in my hands. Can you even imagine the responsibility? Nobody should wield that kind of power. Nobody. Not me, boy, and certainly not you, either. Our knowledge has to be preserved, but it has been secret for ages, and rightly so. Because making it publicly known would change the world forever, and it would bring us into a position we can't possibly handle. Always remember that."

And Robyn had remembered. In all those years, he had never even been tempted to go against Nichasin's warning. Until now. "You ... you have no idea what you're suggesting," he said hoarsely, looking Jonis directly in the eyes, not even caring if the older man saw his distress. "If I do this, there will be no going back. There will be no peace, not ... not ever."

Jonis held his gaze. There was still pity in his eyes, but there was steel, too. Robyn realized that the steward was, in fact, perfectly aware what he was asking of Robyn.

"We'll all stand by your side," Jonis said quietly.

Robyn laughed, realizing that it sounded dangerously close to hysteria. "If I do this, nobody will be able to protect me," he said.

"And if you don't do this, nobody will be able to protect the castle," Jonis replied, still quiet, steely quiet.

Robyn, in the middle of coming up with an angry response, paused. He thought of his mother, his young siblings, of everybody in the castle. That was the other side of the truth, the one Nichasin hadn't mentioned. Suddenly, Robyn felt lonelier than he ever had in his life, realizing with absolute certainty that no matter what he did, in the end, he would have to face the consequences, and when it came to that, nobody would be able to help or protect him. There were many people who cared about him, who only wanted his best, but they couldn't help him now, couldn't take this choice or its consequences from him.

He felt something inside him turn to ice. It was a scary feeling, but it was liberating, too, filling him with resolve. There was no going back, no hiding, so he had no choice but to be strong.

He looked up at Jonis, taking a deep breath. "All right, then," he said. Nothing more, because what else was there to be said?

***

As the sun rose the next morning, Robyn was once more standing on the castle's highest tower. This time, however, he was not going to be a passive observer. He hadn't slept a minute that night, but he felt no tiredness now, his body

Robyn's Gift

filled with an energy that wasn't his, yet ready to do his bidding.

In the enemy camp, people were beginning to stir, to get ready for another assault. This time, however, they were in for a brutal surprise, for forces they couldn't even begin to understand.

Hardly feeling the sun's warmth, Robyn withdrew inside himself, concentrating on what Nichasin had taught him in years of patient study. This time, it counted, but Robyn knew that he could do it, that the Arcane powers would not desert him. A strange bluish light began to glow in his outstretched right hand as he muttered the age-old incantation.

The End

Escape!
by Michelle Proulx

Rhapsody Swansong, teenage bard-in-training, was having an extraordinarily bad day.

Having forgotten to set her alarm charm the previous night, she'd woken up exactly seventeen minutes before the end-of-year exam was scheduled to start. Cursing, she fell out of bed, stumbled to her feet, pulled on a dragonhide jacket and leather breeches, and hopped down the spiral staircase whilst attempting to lace up her boots.

As she dashed through the great hall toward the grand double doors leading out to the courtyard, she caught sight of her father—the headmaster of the Ascalon Academy of Arcane Arts and Adventuring—approaching. Rhapsody grimaced, and briefly considered how much trouble she would get into if she pretended she didn't see him. *A lot,* she decided.

"Rhapsody! A word."

Sighing, she skidded to a halt and waited.

"Why are you running late?" her father demanded when he reached her.

"I overslept."

Escape!

"This is not a good start to the day. Your exam is not something to be taken lightly—in fact, it will be extremely difficult. Need I remind you that you *must* pass in order to move on with your studies next fall?"

"Yes, Father. I'm prepared."

"I hope that's true. Since you are my daughter, everyone is expecting you to do well. *I* am expecting you to do well."

"So am I, Father."

"Good," he said. "Because if I am forced to use my influence as headmaster to secure you a passing grade, I will be disappointed. *Very* disappointed."

"I understand, Father."

"Go," he said, tilting his chin toward the grassy courtyard.

"Thank you, Father," Rhapsody said, and fled.

She raced through the open doors, down the stone steps, and out into the morning sunshine. A temporary wooden stage holding a large bronze gong had been constructed in the center of the courtyard. Encircling the stage were several dozen free-standing wooden doors, which teams of students had gathered around as they waited for the exam to start.

Spotting her boyfriend, Nigel, standing near a door carved with frolicking deer, Rhapsody hurried over to greet him. But she paused when she saw who was with him—two paladins-in-training, Jocelyn and Mortimer, and a fire mage named Humphrey who annoyed her to no end.

"What's going on?" Rhapsody asked Nigel as she reached his side. Tilting her head toward Humphrey, she added, "What's *he* doing here? I thought the teams were groups of four, not five."

"They are," Humphrey said, smirking.

"But there are *five* of us here."

"Didn't your boyfriend tell you?" the fire mage taunted.

Rhapsody shot Nigel a questioning look.

The chisel-jawed fighter-in-training winced. "I've been meaning to tell you for a while now. I just haven't found the right way …"

"Tell me *what*?" she prompted.

"Humphrey's in. And you're out. Sorry."

Rhapsody managed to keep calm for exactly three seconds before she exploded.

"You want *Humphrey* instead of me?" she demanded. "*Really?*"

"He's excellent at fire magic."

"He's also a crackpot!"

"I am *not* a crackpot," Humphrey protested. "Why does everyone keep saying that?"

Escape!

"Because you're convinced you're the reincarnation of Magmos the fire drake," Rhapsody snapped. *And because you don't bathe,* she added silently.

"I *am* the reincarnation of Magmos the fire drake," Humphrey said. "He came to me in a dream and promised I would one day cleanse this world with fire and flame."

Nigel rubbed the heel of his hand against his eyes. "Humphrey, shut up. You're not helping. Rhapsody, can I speak to you privately?"

"This had better be good," she muttered.

He grasped her elbow gently and pulled her a few yards away from the others. "Dearest," he began in a soothing tone, "I know you're upset, but you must calm down. You're blowing this way out of proportion."

"I'm blowing this to a perfectly reasonable proportion," she said, wrenching her arm back. "You just kicked me out of our group! I have every right to be furious."

"It's not like we deliberately set out to exclude you," Nigel defended. "Rhapsody, you know how beautiful, witty, and wonderful I think you are. It's just that I'm not sure how much *use* you'll be in the exam. After all, as a bard, your magic lies in your music—and darling, you play the *great harp*. You can't exactly carry one of those into the exam, can you?"

"Of course not. They're massive."

"That's precisely my point," Nigel said. "What use could we possibly have for a bard with no instrument?"

Rhapsody didn't know if she should laugh or cry. "And what am I supposed to do now? I don't have a group, and I certainly can't take the exam on my own."

"I've already taken care of that. I signed you up with a different group—they're right over there."

He pointed at a trio of teenagers gathered beside a door carved with birds in flight. They were a motley bunch—certainly not the sort of people with whom Rhapsody typically associated. The boy in the gleaming chain armor looked fairly well bred, but the girl's brown robes were ill fitting and moth eaten, and the boy in the leather jerkin and knee-high boots had a shady look about him.

Rhapsody glanced at them askance. "Nigel, you can't be serious."

"I know things look grim, dearest, but this is all for the best."

"*How?*"

"Because this arrangement will ensure I pass the exam," Nigel said. "And you're the headmaster's daughter, so you'll pass by default. Then we can spend a romantic summer at my lake house in the Mistvale Mountains, and come next semester you'll have forgotten this ever happened. What do you say?"

Escape!

Rhapsody had several things to say, none of which were very ladylike. But before she could select the most scathing retort, Nigel kissed her on the cheek and said, "I'm glad you're willing to see reason, dearest. Good luck!"

She glowered at Nigel's back as he went off to rejoin his group. *First my father, now my boyfriend,* she thought. *Why is everyone convinced I'm useless? I may not wield the devastating power of arcane fire, or be skilled at swinging around a pointy bit of metal, but I have plenty of other talents. How do I make them see that?*

The answer hit her almost immediately. *I need to ace the exam,* she realized. *That way I can prove to Father I'm capable of passing without his help, and I can enjoy seeing the stunned look on Nigel's face when I beat his score.*

With a determined spring to her step, Rhapsody strode across the courtyard toward her new team. The trio of students looked up as she approached.

"I am Rhapsody Swansong, bard-in-training," she announced. "Thank you for letting a stranger join your group on such short notice."

The shady-looking guy laughed. "You're hardly a stranger."

"I'm sorry, have we met?"

"You're the headmaster's daughter. Everyone knows who you are."

"Ah. Right." Rhapsody paused to regain her composure. "It seems you have me at a disadvantage. You know my name, but I don't know yours."

"Max Weston." He pulled a dagger from a concealed sheath and danced it along his knuckles. "Rogue."

"I'm Lizzy Weston," said the girl in the tattered robes. "Mage."

Rhapsody could easily spot the familial resemblance—they both had messy brown hair and hazel eyes and shared the same lanky build. "Siblings?"

"Twins," Lizzy said.

"I got the looks and the brains," Max said. "She got whatever was left. So, not much."

"Keep telling yourself that," Lizzy said, elbowing him in the arm. Max yelped in mock pain, and she giggled.

The young man in chain mail stepped forward. "I am Gared Montgomery," he said, his hand resting on the hilt of the mace at his waist. "Cleric."

Rhapsody arched an eyebrow, impressed. "Surely not of *the* Montgomerys?"

"I don't like to talk about my family."

She looked closer at him. "If you're a cleric, where's your holy symbol?"

"If you're a bard, where's your instrument?" Gared countered.

Escape!

"I play the great harp. And yes, it has already been pointed out to me how impractical an instrument it is. But don't change the subject—your holy symbol?"

"I don't have one. I'm an atheist."

Rhapsody stared at him. "You're an atheist cleric?"

"That's right."

"An *atheist* cleric."

"You seem to be having trouble with this concept."

"Because it doesn't make any sense! How can you not believe in the gods? They *literally* walk amongst us. My father had dinner with the goddess of woodland ponds and rivulets just last week—she even brought us a fruitcake!"

"It's not that I doubt the existence of the gods," Gared said. "I just choose not to worship them. They've never done anything for me, so why should I do anything for them?"

The stroke of a gong reverberated through the courtyard, cutting off Rhapsody's incredulous response. She looked up at the stage and saw her father standing there, holding a mallet in one hand, gazing out imperiously at the students. The hum of conversation quickly died down.

"The exam will commence shortly," the headmaster announced. "When I give the signal, you will step through your assigned doorways. Each doorway is a portal that leads to a pocket dimension. The portals are one-way only. Your goal is to escape the other dimension by finding an exit portal, which will return you here. Grades will be assigned based on the speed of your escape. If you have not escaped after one hour, you will automatically fail. Any questions?"

Silence from the assembled students.

"The exam begins now. Good luck."

He struck the gong again, and the doors swung open in unison, revealing prismatic portals that glimmered in the morning sunlight. Rhapsody wasn't the closest one to their door, but her teammates weren't making any moves toward it, so she squared her shoulders and strode into the portal.

For several seconds all she could see were shards of rainbow light, shattering and re-forming in a spiralling void around her. Then she stepped out into a small, square room. Yellow light cast by torches in brackets flickered across the stone ceiling, walls, and floor. Rhapsody couldn't see any doors or windows, although there were some furnishings—a table and chairs and assorted wooden bookcases and cabinets. She took a few more steps into the room so her teammates wouldn't crash into her when they arrived.

A few seconds later, Lizzy appeared. As the mage smoothed her frayed robes, she said, "So does the hour start right away, or do you think we have a few minutes to—"

Max practically fell out of the portal and crashed into his sister. Rhapsody winced as the pair tumbled to the flagstones in a mess of limbs and muffled curses.

Escape!

Gared came through last, and the swirling colors of the portal spiralled in behind him and disappeared with a soft *pop*. He looked down at the twins, still struggling to untangle themselves, and sighed. "Again, Max?" He reached down to grab the boy's arm and yank him off Lizzy.

"It's not my fault I'm clumsy," Max protested.

A clumsy rogue? Rhapsody thought glumly. *Just my luck.*

As Gared assisted Lizzy to her feet, Max looked around and said, "Okay, so we're in a big stone box. That means there has to be a secret door somewhere."

"Let's spread out and search," Rhapsody suggested. "And while we do that, Lizzy, why don't you cast *reveal magic* and see if you can find the door that way? Might be faster."

"I don't know *reveal magic*," Lizzy said.

"Oh?" Rhapsody said, confused. "But I thought that was one of the first spells you learned as a mage."

"It is," Lizzy agreed. "For most people. But I, uh ... I only know how to cast one spell."

With a sense of foreboding, Rhapsody asked, "Which one?"

"*Create magic item.*"

"Oh. Well, that's not so bad."

"It is, actually. Because I can't choose what item I create."

"Not at all?"

"No, not at all," Max said flatly. "She has no control whatsoever. Three months ago she tried to create a *cloak of agility* for me. When I put it on, instead of making me more agile, it turned me into a mahogany end table. I spent three days decorating the common room before she figured out how to turn me back."

A mage who can't control her magic. A clumsy rogue. An atheist cleric. And me, a bard without an instrument, Rhapsody thought despairingly. *We're doomed.*

***

Ten minutes later, Rhapsody and her group had yet to find the secret door. They had, however, collected a variety of random items from around the room, including a book on hedge maintenance, a copper pot caked with lard, a letter opener shaped like a tuna, and an ivory-handled mirror inscribed with runes.

"Can anyone read these runes?" Max asked, picking up the mirror and examining it. "They could mean something important."

Lizzy peered over his shoulder. "I think they're written in Draconic."

"Yeah? What do they say?"

Escape!

"How should I know? Do I look like a dragon to you?"

"In the right light …"

Lizzy smacked Max's arm with the back of her hand.

As Max sniggered to himself, Rhapsody said, "I can read Draconic."

When her teammates all looked surprised, she snapped, "What? Bards don't just sit around playing instruments all day, you know. We have other skills."

"Such as?" Max prompted.

Rhapsody snatched the mirror from him. "Such as translating these runes, which I note none of the rest of you can do. Now, everyone be quiet so I can concentrate."

After perusing the jagged symbols for a few moments, she declared, "It says, '*The grave reveals many truths.*'"

"Maybe the mirror reflects the truth?" Lizzy suggested. "Can we only see the secret door as a reflection?"

Rhapsody angled the mirror toward each wall in turn, but no secret door appeared.

"What about the 'grave' part?" Max said. "Maybe we have to dig to find the secret door."

"Through solid stone?" Lizzy countered.

Max shrugged.

Gared took the mirror from Rhapsody, a thoughtful look on his face. "I'm sure I've heard that phrase before," he said.

"Was it in a holy book? No ... wait! I remember now. It was an unholy book—the *Tome of the Undying*."

"Isn't that the book necromancers use to summon zombies?" Rhapsody asked.

Gared nodded. "My Defense Against the Necromantic Arts professor was telling us about it the other day. She said many people misinterpret that phrase—they think it refers to a physical grave, but it actually refers to the *darkness* of the grave."

"Oh," Rhapsody said. Then, "Oh!" She snapped her fingers. "Put out the torches!"

They hurried to extinguish the torches, and the room plummeted into near darkness. The only light came from the mirror in Gared's hand, which glowed a soft green. Rhapsody could see the room reflected in the glass—specifically, the wall behind her, which had a glowing green outline that looked suspiciously like a door.

"It worked!" she exclaimed, and pointed. "The door's there!"

"I'll open it," Max said, starting toward the wall. Halfway there, he tripped on a chair leg and tumbled to the floor, cursing.

While Lizzy giggled, Gared sighed and said, "Never mind. I'll do it."

Escape!

As Max picked himself up off the floor, the cleric ran his fingers along the grooves between the stone wall blocks. After a few seconds, Rhapsody heard a soft *click*. A large section of the wall shifted back and slid aside, and torchlight streamed into the dark room from the chamber beyond.

Rhapsody stepped forward and peered into the new room, which was a much larger version of the first—basically, a square, stone box. At the center of the room sat a large wooden chest secured with a shiny brass lock. "Let's go," she said, and led the way inside.

As soon as all her teammates had followed her through the doorway, the wall slid shut behind them, closing with a loud *thud*. "I hope we didn't need anything from the last room," Lizzy said. "Like a key for that chest."

"We don't need a key," Max said. "We have me. Step aside, law-abiders. Let the rogue do what rogues do best."

He pulled a set of lock-picking tools from his leather jerkin, crouched in front of the brass padlock, and set to work. Thirty seconds later, Rhapsody heard a metallic *snap*. Max cursed.

Lizzy sighed. "Broke the lock pick?"

"I have a spare," Max said, scowling. He dropped the broken tool and pulled another from his kit.

A minute later, that one snapped too. Max threw the pick to the floor with disgust and stood up, shaking his head.

Michelle Proulx

"I never even wanted to be a rogue," he moaned. "I wanted to go to the Royal Chef School so I could cook for kings!"

Rhapsody blinked. "You wanted to be a *chef*?"

"Of course I did—who wouldn't? But mother insisted I come here and train for a proper adventuring profession. So I chose the only class that would let me learn how to use knives."

"Rogue," Lizzy supplied.

"I'm actually really good with my knife," Max said. "It's all the other rogue stuff I can't manage."

"Can your knife open that lock?" Gared asked.

"No."

"Then I suggest we focus on the exam and save our personal stories for later," the cleric said gruffly, and pulled out his mace. "Maybe I can get it open with this."

Rhapsody darted in front of the chest, spreading her arms wide. "No! What if it's booby-trapped?"

"You're being paranoid."

"I'm not," she insisted. "Haven't you ever heard of Alaric the Overly Aggressive? He tried to smash open a chest, but in doing so he broke a vial of acid that destroyed the ancient scrolls inside."

Gared sighed and hooked the mace back onto his belt. "Fine. What do you suggest, then?"

"What about using one of your holy spells?"

Escape!

"I don't cast spells. That requires asking the gods for help, and I don't want to be in their debt."

Rhapsody crossed her arms. "So you're telling me all you really do is hit things with your mace? Why not train to be a fighter instead?"

"Family tradition. Apparently I have 'a natural connection to the divine,' like my father and grandmother, so I have to train to be a cleric. My parents wouldn't have paid for my studies otherwise."

Rhapsody said nothing. She knew what it felt like to have an overbearing parent.

"You know," Lizzy said, "*I* could try to get the chest open."

"No!" Max and Gared chorused instantly.

Rhapsody frowned. "Do either of you have a better idea? I certainly don't."

"She has no control over her magic," Gared said. "We need a less risky solution."

"At least let me try!" Lizzy said. "I'm as much a part of this team as you are."

Rhapsody sent Lizzy an encouraging smile. "Never mind them. Go for it."

As Max muttered under his breath about this being "*such* a bad idea," Lizzie stepped toward the chest. She took a deep breath and held her hands in front of her, as though cradling a large ball. A golden glow enveloped her hands—when she clapped them together, there was a brilliant flash of light.

As the spots cleared from Rhapsody's vision, she saw Lizzy was now holding a slender rod, about ten inches long and translucent and shiny.

"What does it do?" Rhapsody asked. "It looks like it's made of ice."

Lizzy shrugged. "Your guess is as good as mine."

"My father has an enchanted rod," Gared said. "His is red and engraved with flames and shoots fire. Maybe this one shoots ice?"

"If it does," Rhapsody said, "we might be able to shatter the lock with it."

"Test it on the wall first," Gared advised. "Just in case."

Lizzy pointed the rod at the far wall and flicked her wrist. A stream of icicles shot out, shattering against the wall and covering it with a thin sheen of frost.

"Okay, it might work," Rhapsody said. "So, everyone stand back while—"

She was cut off by a loud cracking sound, like a small glacier splitting in two. As the four students watched, gaping, the frosted wall started to shimmer and vibrate. Suddenly, a huge paw with three-inch-long black claws shot out, as if phasing through the wall from an alternate

Escape!

dimension. The paw was followed by an arm, then a leg, and then the rest of the creature—a huge, furry, white, bipedal beast with serrated tusks and hellish red eyes.

"Oh, come *on*!" Lizzy shouted, scrambling backward. "One single useful item that won't accidentally murder us! That's all I ask for!"

Gared reached for his mace, and Max slid his dagger from its sheath.

Rhapsody pulled out the stiletto knife she kept hidden in her boot. "Anyone know what that thing is?" she gasped.

"I'm pretty sure it's a yeti," Lizzy said.

"Why would you summon a yeti?"

"I didn't mean to!"

The yeti's eyes locked on them. It emitted a low, rumbling growl that raised the hairs on the back of Rhapsody's neck.

"We have to fight," Gared said, stepping forward and raising his mace. "I'll engage from the front. Max, flank it and sneak attack from the rear. Rhapsody, protect Lizzy."

The cleric took a deep breath and then lunged at the yeti as it lumbered across the room to meet him head-on. Meanwhile, Max moved toward the wall and started to edge around behind the creature.

Gared managed to smash his mace into the yeti's shoulder, but that only seemed to anger it. Lifting one massive paw, it lashed out and sent him flying back. He hit the wall and tumbled to the floor, groaning. Rhapsody started toward Gared to help him stand, but he was already pushing himself back to his feet, using the mace as a crutch. With an incoherent battle cry, he threw himself at the yeti once more.

While the cleric was holding the beast's attention, Max had managed to maneuver in behind it. He raised his dagger to strike. Just as Gared blocked another of the yeti's crushing blows with his mace, Max darted forward and slashed at the back of the creature's right leg, severing the tendons behind its knee.

The monster howled and stumbled but kept its footing. Then it turned its glowing red eyes on Max and raised its paw. Max dodged to avoid the attack, but tripped on a piece of rubble. The yeti's claws tore across the front of the rogue's leather jerkin, leaving behind four bloody tracks.

"Max!" Lizzy screamed.

As Max collapsed, Gared waved his mace above his head. "Hey! Monster! Over here!"

I feel so useless! Rhapsody thought. *If only I had my harp. Why couldn't I have chosen a more portable instrument? Stupid!*

The yeti lumbered toward Gared again. "Lizzy," Rhapsody said, "you need to make more magic items."

Escape!

Lizzy shook her head, her face white. "Not a chance. My brother's probably already dead because of me—I don't want to kill you and Gared too!"

"He's not dead. Look, you can see his chest moving. But we're all going to be that yeti's lunch soon enough if we don't do something. So ... do something!"

Lizzy opened her mouth, paused, then closed it. "You're right. I can't possibly make things worse, can I?"

"I don't think things get much worse than a rampaging yeti in a locked room," Rhapsody agreed.

The mage nodded and raised her hands. This time, when she clapped, the flash of light revealed a staff. It was black as obsidian and had a glowing red ruby at the tip.

"Now what?" Lizzy asked.

"Point it at the yeti, and shoot!" Rhapsody cried.

"Shouldn't we test it first?"

The monster had Gared pinned against the far wall and was poised to strike a massive blow with its claws.

"There's no time!"

Rhapsody grabbed the staff and pointed it at the monster. A beam of red light shot out, striking the yeti in the center of its back. It roared in pain and staggered, releasing Gared. For a few seconds it just stood in place, convulsing. Then there was a sizzling, popping sound, like a torch spluttering to life. The yeti flung its arms out wide as flames enveloped its shaggy white fur.

"Good shot!" Lizzy said.

But as Rhapsody watched the yeti, she realized its fur wasn't burning—it was *becoming* flames. The creature turned toward her. Its black claws and teeth had transformed into wedges of molten lava, and its eyes burned like hellfire. When it opened its mouth and roared again, a jet of fire shot out.

"Did we just make a … *fire* yeti?" Lizzy said uncertainly.

"I think we did," Rhapsody said. "Whoops."

"How am I supposed to fight this thing now?" Gared demanded as the creature turned back toward him, leaving black scorch marks on the floor.

"We're working on it," Rhapsody called, then rounded on Lizzy. "Quick! Make more items. As many as you can. One of them *has* to be useful."

"I'm not sure that's a good id—"

"Do it!"

Gared valiantly held off the fire yeti while Lizzy created magic items as quickly as she could, dropping them in a small pile at Rhapsody's feet. Most of the items were wearable objects, like rings, hats, or boots—Rhapsody discarded those, concerned they might curse whoever wore

Escape!

them. But there were also a few rods, which she gathered up and tested on the stone wall.

The first rod did absolutely nothing. The second rod transformed one of the stone blocks into a freshly baked apple pie. Rhapsody immediately used that rod on the yeti, but it didn't seem to have any effect. The third rod produced a stream of acrid smoke—useless. The fourth made a loud *ribbit* sound. Cursing, Rhapsody tossed all the rods aside.

"Here," Lizzy said wearily, handing her a copper ring.

Rhapsody was prepared to drop it straight into the discard pile when she noticed engraving on the outside of the band. Looking more closely, she saw it was carved to resemble an owl in flight. *I know this ring,* she thought. *But how?*

Then it hit her. *The Ballad of Alma Ras! The elf queen with the magical ring of wisdom!* It had been one of the first songs she'd learned to play on her great harp.

"Put this on," she said, shoving the ring at Lizzy.

"No way. I don't want to be an end table."

"It's not going to turn you into an end table," Rhapsody said with more confidence than she felt. "It's a *ring of owl's wisdom*. I think. Put it on!"

Lizzy hesitated.

"Now!" Rhapsody shouted. "Unless you'd rather watch us all get flambéed by the yeti!"

The mage flinched, then grabbed the ring and shoved it onto her finger.

"Well?" Rhapsody asked anxiously. "Did it work?"

The panic slowly vanished from Lizzy's eyes, replaced with cool calm. "It did," she said. "Everything is suddenly so clear to me."

"Hey!" Gared shouted, ducking low to dodge a swipe from the yeti—the flaming paw left singe marks on his cheek. "I could really use some help over here!"

"You'll be fine in a minute," Lizzy called back.

"He will?" Rhapsody said. "How?"

"Because now I know exactly where I've been going wrong with my magic. I thought I was too weak to cast spells properly, but my problem was actually that I was throwing too much power into them—sort of like trying to squeeze a behemoth into a breadbox."

"And how does that help us?"

"I'm getting there," Lizzy said serenely. "Now that I realize what I've been doing wrong, it should be a simple matter to regulate my power properly and attain control over my spellcasting."

"Wow," Rhapsody said. "That ring really *is* working, isn't it?"

Escape!

"It is," Lizzy agreed. Her hands flashed, and when the light faded, a great harp sat in front of her. "I believe you have need of this?"

As Rhapsody gaped at the glittering instrument, Gared bellowed in pain—the yeti had scorched an angry red line along the side of his neck. Snapping out of her stupor, the bard hurried forward and began to play.

Rhapsody might not have much skill at fighting, but no one could dispute she was an excellent harpist. Her fingers danced along the strings, producing a beautiful, haunting melody that filled the entire room. The enchanted music began to weave a spell of calm around the yeti, bewitching it and causing it to forget all about Gared as it stared, transfixed, at Rhapsody's harp.

The beast's eyelids started to droop, and it hunched forward, as if standing was a great effort. As the music swelled, the fire yeti yawned once, then twice. Then it toppled backward and crashed to the floor, snoring loudly. Its flaming fur smoldered against the flagstones.

Rhapsody stopped playing, and for a few seconds the three students just stood there, staring at their fallen foe. Then Lizzy gasped, "Max!"

She raced past the slumbering yeti—her teammates only steps behind—and crouched beside her brother. When she gently rolled Max onto his back, Rhapsody saw his chest was soaked with blood.

Max's eyelids fluttered open. "Did we ... win?" His breath came out in ragged gasps.

"We did," Lizzy said, reaching out to cradle her twin's cheek with her palm.

"No thanks ... to me," he wheezed.

"You're wrong," Gared said. "If you hadn't crippled that beast, it would have taken off my head long before Rhapsody and Lizzy managed to incapacitate it. You saved us all."

The faintest wisp of a smile passed over Max's lips. "Maybe ... I would have made ... a decent rogue ... after all." Then his eyes rolled back into his head, and he passed out.

"The wound is fatal," Lizzy said bleakly. "He has only minutes left." A tear rolled down her cheek.

Rhapsody felt her own tears begin to well, but forced herself to stay focused. "Can't you make something to heal him?" she asked the mage.

Lizzy shook her head miserably. "Healing magic is divine, not arcane. This is beyond my abilities."

Rhapsody rounded on Gared. "You're the cleric! Help him!"

Escape!

"Not possible," Gared said, his face pale. "I told you, I don't cast spells."

"Don't, or *won't*? Gared, Max is dying!"

Gared took a deep, shuddering breath. Just as Rhapsody thought for sure he would refuse again, his jaw clenched determinedly.

"Okay," he said. "I'll do it. For Max."

He knelt beside Max, splayed his hands over the rogue's bloody chest, and shouted to the heavens, "Heal!"

Nothing happened.

"Heal, dammit!"

Still nothing.

"Maybe you're doing it wrong?" Rhapsody suggested.

"I'm not." Scowling, Gared dropped his hands and glared up at the stone ceiling. "Come on, gods!" he shouted. "You want to hear me say it? Fine. I'm sorry! I'm sorry I dragged you into something that never really had anything to do with you in the first place! I only renounced you to spite my father, because I wanted to hurt him the way he'd hurt me by abandoning his family to run off and serve you!" He hung his head. "I should never have turned my back on you for such a petty reason. I realize that now."

A glowing figure appeared before them. It was a willowy woman in a long blue dress, with flowing hair, crossed arms, and an annoyed look on her beautiful face.

"Stop bellowing, Gared Montgomery," said the woman, her voice like a choir of bells. "I could hear you all the way from the Sapphire Halls."

"Morana, goddess of healing!" he exclaimed, looking up. "Please tell me you're here to help!"

"I am," the goddess said, and raised her hand. "*If* you're willing to give up this 'atheist cleric' nonsense."

"I swear it on my life," Gared said solemnly. "I shall never again forsake the gods."

Morana smiled. "Perhaps there is hope for you yet." She touched her index finger to Gared's forehead. "Your connection to the divine is restored. Do with it what you will. But know that if you stray again, I will not be so forgiving."

"Understood," Gared said, bowing his head. "Thank you, my lady."

The goddess nodded graciously, then shimmered out of sight as quickly as she had appeared.

Gared spread his hands across Max's chest once again. "Heal!" he cried.

A silvery light enveloped the rogue as the healing magic spread through his body, knitting his torn flesh back together and replenishing his lost blood. A few moments later, his eyelids fluttered open. "Ow," he moaned.

Lizzy threw her arms around her brother.

Escape!

"I just said 'ow!'" Max protested.

As the twins squabbled, Rhapsody turned to Gared. He had stood up and stepped back a few feet, as if not to intrude on the family reunion. She joined him and nudged his arm with hers. "You did good."

"So did you," Gared said. He paused. "Except for the whole 'fire yeti' thing. That was you, right?"

"It's possible I should have tested the staff before using it on the yeti," Rhapsody admitted, smiling sheepishly. "Sorry about that, by the way. You look like you just walked through a bonfire."

"Don't worry about it," Gared said. "We've all made mistakes today. But we're still alive, so let's call it a victory, shall we?"

Rhapsody laughed. "I can get on board with that." Suddenly, she gasped. "Oh no!"

"What is it?" Gared demanded.

"The exam! We still have to escape!"

***

After their epic battle with the fire yeti, the rest of the exam felt almost too easy by comparison. Still, the fight had set them back considerably, so they had to scramble to make up for lost time.

The sleeping beast's flames had charred the side of the chest just enough that they could pry the boards apart. Inside the chest, they found a trapdoor in the floor. They lowered themselves through into a large chamber with a pool of water. After spending several minutes fighting off a school of mermaids who tried to drag them under and drown them, they discovered an exit tunnel inside a giant clamshell at the bottom of the pool. There were a few more rooms after that—all with a trick or trap they had to overcome to move forward. By the time they found the exit portal and stepped through, they had only minutes to spare before the hour was up.

Rhapsody didn't even have a chance to breathe a sigh of relief that they'd made it back to the courtyard in time before one of the professors walked up to them.

"You four are a mess," he said, frowning. "Scorch marks, ripped clothes … Did you manage to set off every single trap in there?"

"Not *every* trap," Rhapsody said. She didn't mention the fire yeti, as it would have definitely caused Lizzy to fail.

The professor sighed and shook his head. "Well, you managed to escape in the allotted time—*barely*—so I do have to pass you. But I'm not impressed. Let's try for a better showing next semester, hmm?"

"Yes, sir," they chorused contritely.

As the professor moved on to grade the next team, Lizzy leaned against the doorframe of their portal and looked at her

Escape!

teammates. "Thank goodness that's over," she said, and twisted the *ring of owl's wisdom* around her finger. "I've heard it said that near-death experiences sometimes make you re-examine your priorities. Anything about your life you want to change?" She shot a meaningful look at her brother.

Max scratched his chin thoughtfully. "You know," he said, "I think there is. When we get home, I'm going to have another talk with Mother about going to chef school. It's been almost a year since I last brought it up—maybe I can get her to see reason this time." He laughed. "If I can handle being nearly disembowelled by a fire yeti, I'm pretty sure I can handle her screaming at me about 'ruining my life' and 'wasting my potential.'"

"It can't hurt to try," Lizzy agreed, smiling.

"Yeah, you just need to …" Rhapsody trailed off as she noticed Nigel standing with his team beside the stage. "Hold that thought. I'll be right back."

"Where are you going?" Gared asked.

"To have a long-overdue talk with my boyfriend."

As she strode across the courtyard toward Nigel, she could hear him regaling a small circle of admiring students with tales of his daring—and undoubtedly made-up—exploits during the exam. When Rhapsody waved her hand to catch Nigel's attention, he excused himself from the group and came to meet her.

"There you are, dearest," he said, smiling. But his smile faded as he surveyed her dishevelled appearance. "Ah. I take it you didn't pass. Well, I suppose that was to be expected. Don't worry, your father will—"

"We're through, Nigel," Rhapsody said.

He stared at her. "What?"

"I'm breaking up with you," she said firmly.

"You are? But why?"

"Because you have no faith in me, and I deserve better than that. So, we're done."

"But you can't break up with me!" Nigel protested. "I'm a duke's son! I'm fabulously wealthy! Not to mention handsome, and charming, and perfect! You'll *never* find someone as good as me."

"Maybe not. But at least it won't be you."

Rhapsody's heart was pounding, but she felt strangely calm—she knew she'd made the right decision. She turned on her heel and marched back across the courtyard as Nigel continued to yell protestations after her.

"So," Rhapsody said brightly as she rejoined her team. "Time to celebrate?"

"I'm always up for a party," Max said. "What did you have in mind?"

"Well, I have a tower suite—one of the perks of being the headmaster's daughter. Shall we go there?"

Escape!

"Sounds good to me," Gared said.

"But what about food and drinks?" Max asked. "A party isn't a party without snacks."

"Drinks are easy," Rhapsody said. "My father has a liquor cabinet in his study, and I know the password to get in. As for food—"

"I've got that covered," Lizzy interrupted, and pulled something from the folds of her robes. It was one of the enchanted rods she'd made during their fight with the yeti.

"You didn't!" Rhapsody exclaimed.

Lizzy grinned. "I did." She twirled the rod in her hand like a baton. "Who wants pie?"

The Twelfth Witch
by Juliana Rew

Tessa riffled through the Help Wanted ads looking for a paying internship. The last six applications had fallen through, and she was thoroughly discouraged and depressed.

So much for family connections, she thought. Her eleven sisters were all more than fully employed, and none of them had ever had to do apprenticeships. It was humiliating. It seemed that at every interview, the Hermetic Resources Specialist just wanted to pepper Tessa with questions about her famous siblings.

"Is it true that Norella and Hyperia can control the weather and stop rivers in their tracks?"

"Um, yes."

"Great Goddesses! Those would be useful skills we could really use. And I hear that Caledonia can play on a golden lyre and charm both young and old into the dancing fire?"

"Right. But technically it's the harp that does all the work."

"Well, witches with their own tools are in demand. Employers don't like to supply them. Most don't really like to train, either. They want someone ready to go on Day One. I've heard that your sister Morgana has her own grisly lindworm?"

"Well, yeah, although I'd call it more of a dragon."

"What a plus! I can hardly wait to hear what you have to offer, Tessa. We're really looking for help in the armaments area, you know, creating a blade that never needs sharpening, or clockwork soldiers that never run down."

"A perpetual motion machine has yet to be invented," Tessa pointed out. "I'm just looking for an internship so I can build my resume while I finish my studies." Companies were always trying to get poor grad students to work for cheap on open questions that even the greatest sorcerers had yet to figure out.

They would prattle on and on like that, right on down the list, until Tessa would finally cut them off, saying, "Yeah, yeah, yeah, their equals have not been seen on the face of the Earth." After that the interview would go downhill.

"We'll call you, Tesseracta," they would say. But they never did.

Tessa buttoned her icy hoodie up over her mail to cover her head against the freshening breeze. It was beginning to snow. Her mother had encouraged her to wear a warm cowl to the interview, but that was just too old-fashioned. You had to suffer a little for beauty. Well, actually, you didn't; it's easy enough to slap on some glamour. She had *some* integrity, for Goddesses' sake.

Flameit, she'd do anything to stop living in her parents' cellar, though she did enjoy the easy access to root-vegetable snacks. The smell of sulfur from her father's lab permeated her clothes, and it was impossible to get it out. But the job market was so bleak, she didn't know when she'd ever be able to get her own place.

On the way home, she had grabbed the latest job openings and had nearly given up on finding anything promising, when her gaze paused on the following:

SOLID INDOOR WORK. NO EXPERIENCE NECESSARY.

That didn't sound too bad. Not many details, though. She flicked a circle around it, sending an inquiry to the advertiser with her qualifications. She settled back to wait, stroking her familiar, Mnemonic Nick. Nick was a miniature dire corgi who could charm the pants off an angry berserker. Irresistible.

"Hey, Esmeralda," she said, giving her crystal mo-ball a shake and turning it over. The die within the ball bobbed briefly, then her best friend's face appeared.

"Hey, Belledame," Esmeralda replied. "How did the interview go?"

The Twelfth Witch

"Total debacle, as usual. I'm getting desperate. My only talent seems to be that I'm a vegetarian. That doesn't seem to bring the headhunters calling."

"Maybe you should become a cook. Your stuffed portobello mushrooms are to die for."

"Thanks. It's the leeks. But no, that's Nigella's bag."

"Have you talked to your advisor? I'd think he could find you something."

"Oh, he's all right, I guess, but I'd just like something more than these internship gigs. . ."

"More what?"

"Crazy."

"Crazy? Like exciting?"

"Yes, but also more cutting edge. And I don't mean keeping blades sharp. I mean really out there, where most people would think it's insane to go. Something new that would make me stand out from the crowd."

"Well, you've got the family genes for it. All your sisters have found a niche. Say, why don't you ask one of them?"

"Definitely not. It's got to be on my own terms."

"Sorry I'm not much help. I'm such a nerd, I just study all the time. Wait, maybe there's something in one of my books. . ."

Just then, the crystal flashed.

"I've got a call coming in, Ezzy. Call you back?" Tessa broke the connection.

"Yes?"

"Tesseracta Rowan?"

"Yes, that's me."

"I'm G. R. Penrus of Marmion Industries. Is this a good time?"

"Yes, certainly. I wanted to talk to you about your job ad."

"You are a fully qualified sorceress, are you not?"

"Of course! You've heard of the Twelve All in Dread, right?"

"Who?"

This was a first. This guy had never heard of the Rowan sisters.

"Um, could you tell me a little about the job? I'm a grad student, so I can't work full time, but I'm willing to take pretty much anything."

"Ah, excellent. You see, we mainly conduct covert operations, so anything we tell you must be held in the strictest confidence."

"No problem."

"In a nutshell, we assist parties desiring to break untenable contracts."

"Like what, for example?"

The Twelfth Witch

"Oh, escaping arranged marriages, runaway-bride rescue, that sort of thing. It's easy work if one is a witch."

"Is this legal?" Tessa asked, a little worried. She could just picture pitchfork-bearing families coming after her after she ruined their fifty-thousand-geltrangg wedding.

"Legality is rarely the issue for our clients."

"I see. You want some poor schlub of a rookie to do your dirty work for you."

"On the contrary. The work requires intelligence and the highest moral character."

"What about experience? Are you going to train me?"

"We expect you to rely on your best judgment. That's why we pay so well. Your credentials are excellent, so we are prepared to make an offer."

He scribbled on a small piece of paper and held it up to the crystal. The figure was a little distorted and blurry, but Tessa was finally able to make it out. Her mouth fell open. The pay was at least double anything she'd ever applied for.

Tessa knew that if something appeared too good to be true, it probably was. The whole thing sounded a little shady to her. But she was ready to try ever more lunatic things if it would get her that one-room forest cottage.

"Count me in, Mr. Penrus. I won't let you down."

"I'm positive about that, Tesseracta. Welcome aboard. Oh, and be sure to bring your armor."

Penrus broke the connection, turned to his secretary, and said, "She seems quite eager."

***

"Penrus Escort and Security Service," said the voice at the other end of the mo-ball. "Please be advised this is not a secure connection."

Tessa hesitated. What was she getting herself into?

"I'm just calling to see when you want me to come in."

"One moment." The sound of lame muzak began to play.

"Tesseracta. Good of you to check in. We've got your first assignment all lined up. It's all in this heroic poem."

Tessa listened as Mr. Penrus described the case.

"You didn't tell me there were dragons involved."

"*Sleeping* dragons," Penrus stressed. "It is your job to make sure they don't awaken."

Right. Well, maybe she could go get some pointers from Morgana, in case the worst should happen. No. She was going to do this herself, and besides, she had her protective spells and armor. Should be a piece of cake. If she aced this assignment, there was even the chance of being promoted into the Twelve. She fancied herself as the greatest of them all—the Twelfth Witch Who Could All Things Understand.

On the pretext of having a date, Tessa borrowed her sister Euphorbia's earth-burrowing coach for the night. It had

The Twelfth Witch

been slow going under the frozen soil, but shortly after midnight she arrived at the castle at last. The bitter chill of December poked inquiring fingers through the joints of her armor. An owl hooted in the trees nearby, sizing up a poor rabbit that limped in the frozen grass. A lone guard sat at the front gate, hunched over a tiny fire and obviously not expecting guests.

"I thought this was going to be indoor work," Tessa muttered, blowing on her hands to get some feeling back. "Best get inside and get it done."

The wedding guests were all within, Tessa knew, most fast asleep after the evening's prenuptial revels. She slipped by the guard with no trouble and entered the courtyard. Taking care not to step in any, she stopped briefly to enjoy the familiar perfume of horse manure and then spotted the arched portal leading to the chapel. That was where tomorrow's wedding would occur, and where the bride would undoubtedly be making her last confessions to the priest before retiring. As quietly as possible, Tessa clanked into the chapel. A pair of carved stone angels stood at the entry, their wings slightly unfurled, eager to enter heaven. Their beady eyes seemed to follow her as she crept in.

Tessa scanned the front pews for the bride. An old woman snored gently in the second row, her face pale. The bride was nowhere in evidence. She must have left the chaperone to doze and gone off to bed. Tessa retraced her steps, exiting the great hall and heading for the sleeping quarters in the north tower.

Working her way down the second-floor corridor, Tessa finally found the bride's chamber. The girl sat bent over in a chair beside the bed, probably reciting one last prayer. Tessa made her move.

"Psst."

The girl started and looked up. She had been crying.

"What? Who are you?"

"I'm the one who's going to get you out of this fix."

"Oh, Lochinvar, I knew you'd come," the girl said. She held out her hands, which had been tied tightly.

I'm not Lochinvar! I'm a girl, for Goddesses' sake! Tessa thought, sticking her chest out. She had to admit, the armor didn't do much for her figure.

Tessa decided that this Lochinvar person was as good a disguise as any. She sawed away at the girl's bonds. "Like I said, I'm just here to take you away from your bloodthirsty relatives."

The girl blushed. This Lochinvar must be pretty hot.

"Did you talk with my father, Lochinvar?"

Brilliant, thought Tessa. "Let's go. Your true love is waiting."

The Twelfth Witch

"But it's a holy day," the girl protested. "St. Agnes's Eve."

"Don't worry about your reputation. Any who look upon us will see only your chaperone," Tessa said.

"Wait. You're not Lochinvar—you're a witch!" exclaimed the girl, opening her mouth to call for help but then thinking better of it.

"Tessa. Pleased to make your acquaintance," Tessa said, shaking her by the hand.

"I'm Maddy," the girl said. Suddenly Maddy's eyes widened slightly. Tessa twisted a bit to take a look, just enough to receive a glancing blow from the side. She fell to her knees in pain.

She must have blanked out temporarily, because when she awoke, she was lying on the ground looking up at a brown-robed priest with his foot on her throat.

"Aha, we've got you now, Lochinvar," he said. He held a heavy chalice in his hand. Tessa's tongue probed her rapidly swelling lip, tasting the metallic tang of sanguine fluid.

"Aagh," she said.

He lifted the cup to strike Tessa again. She struggled to escape, but the heavyset man had her pinned. Tessa glanced at her gauntlet, which was barbed with sharp spikes. She glanced at the priest's sandaled foot and made the obvious connection.

As the priest hopped about howling in pain, Tessa clambered to her feet. The angry man rushed at her again, and she held out her hands, grabbing his cowl and giving him a knee to the groin. She was glad she had taken that self-defense class. But it wasn't enough. It never was. His big hands closed around her neck, easily crushing her gorget and choking her. Hardly able to breathe, she made one last effort, thrusting her clasped hands upward to break his hold. As his hands flew away, she stood with her arms outstretched, and chanted. She wished to be rid of this troublesome priest.

The cleric's bulky brown robe disappeared, leaving him naked. He shrieked in embarrassment and did his best to cover his previously private parts. Then chunks of his face began to melt as if his skin had been removed, but there was no blood. His bones gradually disappeared, leaving only his internal muscles and brain dangling in the air. She was somehow sending parts of him *otherwhen*. What had she been chanting? Oh, yes, a begone spell. The last of the man disappeared with a pop. He had probably gone to the future—or the past—and she had no idea when or if he'd be back.

Tessa grabbed the horrified Maddy, and they headed down the stairs of the tower, checking over their shoulders

The Twelfth Witch

all the way. Tessa opened the door and propelled Maddy into the courtyard.

"Aarreeyah!" A dragon was chained to the front gate, barring their exit.

Tessa cursed under her breath. She should have prepared better. Even her full battle armor was ineffective against dragons. Theirs was the oldest magic.

She still had a splitting headache from when the priest had clocked her. What should she do?

"Umm, Maddy, why don't you go on back upstairs while I take care of this?"

Shaking, Maddy nodded. She turned and ran for the tower door.

"And watch out for the priest," Tessa called.

Her shout drew the dragon's attention, and it let loose a tongue of red-gold flame, just as a warm up. It would be pretty if it weren't so lethal.

"Nice draggy," Tessa called to draw the dragon away. She pulled out her sword and edged backward. Too late. Suddenly she was engulfed in flames. She dived behind a low stone wall, displacing sacks of sand and tossing them out into the courtyard.

Now she felt sheepish, getting roasted after traipsing unprepared into a dragon's keep. She sat down and tried to pull off her helmet, but her hair got caught in the visor, and she spent a painful few moments trying to untangle it. A wad of her black hair still stuck to the pin of the visor, punishment for her impatience. She rubbed her temples and folded her palms over her eyes. Images of fireworks had seared themselves onto her retinas, leaving her with flashbulb eyes.

The feeling of the armor was oppressively hot, so she clumsily undid the side buckles that reached from the waist up to the underarm. There must have been a dozen or more of them. Exhausted, she shed the breastplate and stripped down to her shirt of chain mail, burning her fingers. She ached all over from the night's exertions. She looked at her reflection in the pile of metal. What a mess. Her eyes were bloodshot, she was missing a tooth, and what was left of her hair was matted to her forehead. But mostly, she felt bad for the poor bride. She'd been deranged to take this assignment. She had totally bungled the extraction—and blown her chance at a promotion.

A mighty blast from a horn heralded disaster. *Well, that's it,* she thought. The whole castle would be swarming down on her shortly.

She cowered as the thunder of the dragon's footsteps approached the wall she was hiding behind. She was toast. Well, there was nothing for it except to do to the dragon what she'd done to the priest. . .

The Twelfth Witch

"Sit down and leave her alone, boy." *Morgana?*

Tessa peeked over the wall. Her sister was petting the dragon, feeding the kreatophagous creature treats of an unsavory nature. Her other sister Ettagorn stood nearby, her fingers idly playing over the pistons of her blarebugle.

"You can come out now. The mission's over."

"But I didn't succeed at all," Tessa protested. "The bride's still up there in her room, and everyone's waking up. I'm ashamed you had to come bail me out."

"We didn't bail you out, little sister. While you were creating a diversion, Lochinvar came in and stole her away," Morgana said. "Nice job tesseracting the priest, by the way. Good work."

Good work? Confused but grateful that her sisters had her back, Tessa exhaled and collapsed with a clatter. As she toggled in and out of consciousness, she heard her sister talking to someone on the other end of her mo-ball.

"She'll be fine, Penrus. She's just managed to get herself a little singed. It's no exaggeration when I say I think she has a great future." Although Tessa knew the mission hadn't come off exactly as planned, she appreciated her sister's attempt to bolster her confidence, and it didn't hurt that Morgana was taking this opportunity to engage in a little PR for the Twelve. So, Penrus *had* heard of the Rowan sisters, after all!

"At least she's eager," he replied, not the least bit fooled.

***

"Hmm, this tomato-and-artichoke bruschetta isn't half bad," Tessa's father said, helping himself to another piece. "Must be the olive oil. So, what's this I hear about you getting a job?"

"You left out '*finally*,' Dad," Tessa replied.

"I didn't say that—"

"I suppose Morgana told you about the St. Agnes's Eve fiasco?"

"Well, it's a little hard to miss the new shaved hairdo. Doing the punk thing now, are we?"

"Can't we all just enjoy the lovely dinner Tessa slaved over all afternoon?" her mom piped in.

"I only meant—I just wanted to say that we're proud of you, Tesseracta. We know you can do whatever you put your mind to. You remember that's the twelfth witch's special talent, don't you?"

The grandfather clock bonged deeply in the hall. Tessa set down her fork and looked around. Her parents were positively beaming at her. Home still looked the same, but somehow it felt different—the crazy new something she'd been waiting for was here too.

Tessa was beginning to all things understand.

***

The Twelfth Witch

"Questions?" asked the Great Frakulus, concluding his invited talk at the University. About forty students had trooped over to the Medallion Applied Sciences Building, endowed by the incredibly rich thaumaturgic megalopoly. They all hoped to get jobs with Medallion one day.

"Why do you want to replace phlogiston with natural gas, anyway?"

"Glad you asked. Medallion feels that phlogiston's days are numbered. It's costly to extract and contributes to global warming. People just aren't willing to put their lives on the line for a pound of phlogiston any more. We have entered into an agreement to retrofit the entire dragon fleet with natural gas by next year. It will result in savings of over ten million geltranggs over the life of the contract."

The room burst into cacophonous booing and whistling. Tessa stood up and tried to restore order. She failed utterly, and the students streamed out of the hall muttering and jostling.

Tessa now regretted agreeing to introduce Frakulus while her advisor, Professor Randio, was away attending to pressing business.

"I do have thome projecth here that you could do to make a little ekthtra money," he'd said in his charming Castilian accent. As he stroked his familiar, Gus, Tessa's eyes began to itch and swell. She was deathly allergic to cats. "I realize it'th hard living on a grad thtudent thalary."

Tessa agreed heartily. *I will probably never get out of my parents' cellar in this lifetime.*

"Goddeth bleth you," Randio lisped, scooping up Gus and vanishing.

"That went well, didn't it?" Frakulus said. "That's what happens when you try to keep the public informed."

Tessa apologized and walked with him back to the quad. She waved good-bye as the tall figure twirled his cape and stepped backward into the shimmering freightflinger. He did not wave back.

She'd known the Great Frakulus's work had something to do with energy exploration, but she didn't usually pay much attention to such things. Earth-burrowing activities tended to be more her sister Euphorbia's bag. Besides, her father's experiments generated enough sulfur and gas to keep the household warm all winter. Except her room in the root cellar, alas. Luckily, she spent a lot of time puttering in her parents' kitchen.

***

Dinner was sautéed asparagus with hollandaise, one of Tessa's veggie specialties. Her secret weapon was a dash of Parmesan cheese. As she set the spoon on automatic to prevent the egg yolks from congealing, she mused over the

The Twelfth Witch

afternoon's lecture. Just who was this "contract" with, anyway?

She pulled her crystal mo-ball from her pocket, gave it a shake, and turned it over. Wait until her sister Morgana heard about this. Tessa was pretty sure that nobody would be able to retrofit anything until the Twelve All in Dread approved. Well, they were only the Eleven so far, but someday Tessa hoped to reach her sisters' level of expertise.

The die within the ball bobbed briefly, then Morgana's face appeared. Tessa set the ball beside the stove.

"Hey, Morgana."

"What's up, kiddo?"

Tessa filled her in on Frakulus's seminar about Medallion's northern venture, ending with a breathless question. "So who do you think has this so-called contract?"

"Relax, dear. It's all under control. Except perhaps for the Pure Water Fund people. Penrus and I are negotiating with them now."

"But is it going to be safe for dragons?" Not that Tessa was overly fond of her sister's pets. Absentmindedly, her hand strayed to the bald spot she'd gotten on one side from yanking her red-hot armet off too quickly the other night. She'd been wearing the hood up on her cowlie all week to cover it.

"We'll never know unless we try," Morgana said.

Juliana Rew

Tessa felt a little better knowing that Marmion Industries and her sisters were on top of things. She wondered when, if ever, she'd be in the loop for breaking news.

"Which reminds me," Morgana said, "we'll need an escape clause on the contract if things don't work out." That was Marmion's specialty—covert operations and breaking untenable contracts. So maybe things weren't quite as copacetic as Morgana let on. . .

"What can I do to help? I've got the week off, with Professor Randio off *incommunicado* with something or other."

"We'd like you to go up there and check out the Medallion operation."

"Anything in particular?"

"As Penrus would say, 'we expect you to rely on your best judgment. That's why we pay so well.'"

Tessa started to grimace but decided to maintain a poker face.

"There's my girl," Morgana said, breaking the connection. Tessa flipped the asparagus spears one last time with a spatula and pushed them onto a plate.

***

Kekkonen Park was magnificent, no doubt about it. Just as the Great Frakulus had conjured in his presentation, three

The Twelfth Witch

tall conical mountains like rabbit ears marked the boundaries of the park, surrounding a deep fell in the middle. High clouds stretched through azure skies, casting shadows over the gold-tinged heather. How anyone could allow oil and gas leases on the starkly beautiful moor was beyond her. Nevertheless, she was there to get the lay of the land.

"Hello, young lady," a middle-aged man in a gray felted wool caftan greeted her. "Need a ride?" He pointed to his snowstrider and gestured for her to climb on behind.

"Where to?"

"The Medallion installation, if you please," Tessa said.

"You aren't one of those pesky Rowan sisters, are you?" the man asked.

"Why, yes, how did you know?" She decided not to take umbrage at the word "pesky." She often felt that way about them herself.

"You're not the first one to come poking her nose around here," he replied. "Just make sure you use protection."

I brought my armor, Tessa mused.

"Armor ain't gonna be enough," he said, as if reading her thoughts. "There's been a monster roaming about the fell."

"I'm sure I'll be fine." Tessa sniffed. "Please just get me there, before I look for other transportation."

"All right, hold your horses," he said then took off with whiplash-inducing speed.

Within a few minutes, they pulled up to a chain-link fence topped with barbed wire and posted with signs warning that unauthorized personnel would be prosecuted.

"Thanks," Tessa said, peeling off what she thought was a generous twenty-geltrangg note. The man peered suspiciously at the money, as though it was foreign currency.

"I assure you, it's legal tender everywhere," Tessa said.

He shrugged, and the snowstrider galloped away as if pursued by demons.

Just beyond the Medallion enclosure sat a tall guard tower, apparently empty. Tessa crunched over the permafrost to the gate and pronounced the number Morgana had given her to her mo-ball. There was no answer. "Try again later," the die said. She decided to essay the intercom and leaned in to push the red button. She heard a soft snort as a cold, wet nose poked its way under her hand and pushed it away.

"Aww," she said. "A little reindeer." The waist-high artiodactyl was so adorable that it would give even her familiar, Mnemonic Nick, a run for his money. Her miniature dire corgi was a ten on the cuteness scale. She hoped her best friend Esmeralda was taking good care of him.

The Twelfth Witch

"Lady Tesseracta," the precious creature said, "Lady Greneth sends her greetings." That explained a lot. Greneth could tame all that in the greenwood crept.

"Grenny? She's here?" That was just her luck, flameit. As usual, one of her older sisters had gotten the jump on her.

"We must take care not to be seen. I will escort you through a rear entrance that is obscured by a stand of pines," the reindeer said. "There is something I must show you. Follow me closely."

"Okey doke," Tessa agreed.

"Not that close," it cautioned, pulling up lame.

"Sorry. Here, I'll go clear." She shuddered slightly, and her hoodie turned transparent, totally covering her torso and mail headdress. She crouched behind as the reindeer traced a torturous path designed to mimic random grazing.

"Is this where we'll find Gren?" Tessa asked.

"Shh. Lady Greneth is not here—she merely bade me bring you here."

"Sorry, my bad," Tessa said.

The reindeer shook its head. Apparently it didn't care for bad puns.

Wicked-looking thornbushes camouflaged a short flight of concrete stairs leading to a door into the compound. It was a little strange that there was no fence, but this certainly made things easier. Tessa clanked up the stairs as quietly as her sabatons would permit and pulled it open for the reindeer, but it was already gone.

"I thought you had something to show me. . . Why don't I just go on alone, then?"

She paused as her eyes gradually adjusted to the gloom. Just a big warehouse. No disguised gas wells or anything like that. Palettes lay stacked around the perimeter, probably supplies and construction materials.

Nobody home.

Wait. She heard sounds, like someone crying or moaning. She inched forward. The sounds grew a little louder. Spotting another door, she turned the knob and peeked in. A cry of anguish assaulted her ears, a bloodcurdling noise sufficient to raise a ghost. It was followed by a deafening rumble as the ground shifted under her feet. She scrambled backward. An earthquake? The grinding vibration abruptly subsided.

Her nerve returning, Tessa reopened the door and sought out the direction the sounds were coming from. The dungeon-like room stank of offal, like something the cat had rejected. A cage stood in its center, large enough to hold a prisoner or two, but at first Tessa couldn't see anyone. Suddenly a huge form crashed against the bars, its arms reaching out to claw at her. She stumbled back against a

The Twelfth Witch

wood desk, nearly losing her balance. Claws? Definitely claws.

Tessa's protective spells seemed to be working, because the creature missed by a mile. Nonetheless, she began to see the folly in detouring from her appointed mission. But the desk and chair looked familiar somehow. She magicked open the top drawer. Snacks. Somebody liked Spanish peanuts. The growling grew louder, and she quickly moved on to the next drawer.

Ah, that was more like it. Rolled up maps, blueprints, and assay reports. She quickly stuffed as many as would fit into the front of her cowlie. She should probably get out of there in case there was another temblor.

"May I help you?" a voice boomed behind her. She spun around, spilling a couple of sheepskins. Thank the Goddesses. It was the Great Frakulus.

"Hello, sir, it's me, Tessa, from the university, remember?"

He scowled. "I should have known better than to let Joffrey do that lecture. And now that you've remarked everything, I'm going to have to kill you."

"Remarked everything? But I haven't seen *anything*," Tessa said, "and if I did, I wouldn't even know what it was." So this wasn't Joffrey Frakulus? If not, it must be his twin.

Juliana Rew

"Who are you, anyway?" she asked, when she knew what she should have been doing was sprinting.

The outsize man strode over to the cage and flung it open.

"You're not welcome in *my* legerdomain," he said. "Go get her, Dridfrodril!"

The hulking creature, which was like a cross between a tiger and a bear, screeched and leaped out of the cage, flattening Tessa before she had a chance to think. Things must have gone black for a bit. She awoke to a crushing pressure on her chest. Her eyes itched horribly and felt nearly crusted shut. Eventually she divined that the predator standing on her chest was a feline, its paws denting her cuirass and compromising her breathing. She was deathly allergic to cats. Acid, dander-laden slobber dripped from the fiend's pointed yellow fangs. Tessa's nasal passages grew increasingly febrile, until with an involuntary spasm, her sinuses emptied themselves in a giant explosion.

Begone!

The creature's long furry coat disappeared. It yelped and began shivering. Chunks of raw flesh, eyeballs, and formerly tufted ears melted, along with paws with claws. Bones sheared away, leaving only pulsing organs dangling in the air. Like a drain satisfyingly cleared by a plunger, a final gurgling sound indicated that the ogre had been temporarily

The Twelfth Witch

dispatched to some other dimension. Tessa couldn't be sure when the cat would return, so she began rocking back and forth in an attempt to right herself. Sometimes armor was more trouble than it was worth.

"You killed my familiar!" the man yelled.

"Well, actually …" Tessa began. Just then, a new commotion ensued, and a second Frakulus burst into the room along with several guards. "Seize him," Frakulus Number Two ordered, pointing at his doppelganger with one hand and reaching out to assist Tessa with the other.

"It's little Miss Rowan, if I'm not mistaken." He tugged, and she lurched to a standing position.

The prisoner seemed to shrink before their eyes.

"Who are you, anyway?" Tessa asked again.

"It'th none of your busineth." That lisp was familiar.

"Professor Randio? What are *you* doing here?"

A blinding strobe raked the vault as the professor instantly vanished. Belatedly, Tessa shielded her eyes.

***

Life at the University seemed to go on as usual. Tessa had spent the last two weeks filling in for Professor Randio's Advanced Alchemy class, while the mystery of his disappearance at Medallion Industries' gas refinery retreated to the background. There was still the question of why he had set a beast prowling about the grounds, although it did help explain the lack of staffing around the place. Could it really be true that the shaggy brute was Randio's little tiger cat, Gus?

Her mo-ball signaled an incoming call. "Excuse me," she said to the class. "I've got to take this." She stepped outside and closed the door. It was Morgana.

"Hi, sis. Thought I'd fill you in on the Korvatunturi case. Good work, once again, scoring all those incriminating papers and tesseracting the Fiend of the Fell."

"But Randio escaped, Morgana, nobody knows where. I've failed in *another* mission, if that's what this was."

"Not at all. The documents you appropriated showed that Professor Randio was falsifying the results of the natural gas tests on dragons. Turns out they were a bust, and we're going to have to stick with phlogiston for the time being. Not to mention that all the pumping of frakwater into the wells is increasing seismic activity in the park. Hyperia was all set to stop rivers in their tracks so Euphorbia could tunnel through the earth to construct a pipeline. That's all on hold now, until we can get more data and thoroughly inspect everything for safety. Maybe there's even a scholarly paper in it for you."

"What about the fiend, then?"

"He's had to relocate and become the 'Monster of the Moor' or something. Doesn't have quite the cachet, does it?"

The Twelfth Witch

"Um, okay," Tessa said, willing to take "yes" for an answer.

"Oh, and before I let you go, we need a current picture of you to put in the Grand Hall alongside your sisters. Congratulations, you're officially one of the Twelve now. Talk to you soon."

Tessa'd finally found her special talent. *All things understanding.* She raised her mo-ball up to eye level and turned her head to the side. A nice, dignified profile, perhaps.

"Selfie rampant," she pronounced.

The End

Tartarus Bound
by Kai Herbertz

The Titan hid behind one of the columns lest he be spotted by the patrolling guards. His heart pounded in his chest—the prospect of stealing from the Olympians was both terrifying and exciting. The conversation between members of the patrol grew faint as they moved on to a different section of the palace.

He waited for a while longer until he was sure they were far away enough before proceeding toward his prize. For the heist, he had taken off his footwear in favor of stealth. This precaution entailed a measure of discomfort since the warmth of his body seeped into the cold marble floor beneath him.

Without making a sound he reached a door that towered above him, but the lock was on his level and within reach. Rummaging through his leather coat he produced a set of lock picks from a hidden compartment.

For a moment he considered using an ordinary lock pick to either prove or hone his skill, depending on how long it took to open the door. However, he could not afford to get caught and instead opted for a magical skeleton key. Once inserted into the opening multiple key bits grew from the featureless rod. In a mere moment, the key became a perfect match for the lock. With bated breath the Titan turned the key. Even though he took care not to make any noise, the retreating massive bars on the other side of the door caused an infernal din. At least that was his impression.

The Titan stood hunched over at the door, as if that made him more difficult to see. He looked back and forth with nervous eyes. When no alarm was raised he focused on the door once more. While the noise, which probably sounded louder to him than it actually was, continued, he kept turning the key until it hit resistance.

The Titan withdrew his skeleton key. He placed it back into the secret pocket that was sewn into his coat. With both hands he pushed on the massive door. It swung open with a deafening creak. The room beyond was also lined with white pillars. At the opposite end a few stairs of solid stone led up to a platform, and on it his coveted prize rested: a large dish containing the secret of the gods.

He swallowed because his throat had become dry. Experience as a thief and trickster prevented him from running headlong. He snuck from column to column. At every stop he surveyed his surroundings, looking for traps. As he neared the pedestal he noticed that the pillars next to the stairs bore stone faces that looked directly at the foot of the stairs. He suspected those were magical scrying contraptions and moved out of sight to the rear of the platform.

Jumping up, he grabbed the ledge of the pedestal and hoisted himself up. He stood before the dish in awe. On the inside, the tongues of an ever-burning fire danced. The Titan Prometheus took a vial from his pocket. With a quick swipe he captured the essence of fire. He plopped down the cork onto the vial, satisfied at a job well done.

***

After his escape from Zeus's domain Prometheus steered his sky barque down to Earth. Prometheus moored his boat at a cove and disembarked.

Whistling a happy tune, he sought out a tribe of humans. The creatures looked downright pitiful with their grimy bearded faces. Nevertheless, he looked down on them with the love of a father when they knelt down in front of him.

"Lord Prometheus, you have come," their leader said. Even though their primitive language mostly consisted of grunts, Prometheus could make sense of it. After all, the humans were his proudest creation.

"Rise, my children," he said. "I have brought you a great gift."

As they let out "oh" and "ah" sounds of awestruck admiration he waggled around the vial that held Zeus's fire.

Tartarus Bound

"Tonight we shall feast, for I am going to introduce you to the arcane art of creating fire."

The savage men roared their approval. They led Prometheus back to their village. He listened to and shared their laughter and stories until the hunters returned with the day's game.

Prometheus wasted no time. He showed the men the powerful cleansing properties of fire. Pure undiluted wonder showed in their expressions when they bit down on their first portion of well-cooked meat.

The Olympians looked down on his creation, but he loved these simple creatures with their uncomplicated lives.

After the meal, they laid out the bones as an offering to the gods. Prometheus smiled at that, fond memories of getting the better of Zeus once more on his mind.

Eventually he clapped his hands to draw the attention of the leader. "Your tribe has flourished, and it pleases me to no end that you worship the gods in an appropriate way."

"All thanks to you," the leader said, bowing so far down that Prometheus worried his forehead might touch the ground.

"Today I showed you fire, but I promised more than that. You shall learn how to create fire. There, go get that branch." Prometheus pointed at a tree limb that had broken off and lay on the ground.

The man did not understand, but he obeyed the command. He stood before the fire expectantly.

"Go ahead," Prometheus said. "Hold the branch into the fire."

The man did as he was told, and awestruck chatter rose around him when he walked around with the burning wooden stick.

He allowed the fur-clad wild man to prance triumphantly around the camp, getting used to the flame he carried. Then Prometheus joined him and took the stick from the man. He tossed it into the fire pit. All eyes were on him as he kicked sand onto the fire and smothered the flames.

"What would you do if you didn't have a vial of eternal fire?" he asked the assembled men.

They did not know the answer, of course. He smiled again. His humans were primitive, true, but they were also curious and resourceful. Prometheus knew that they would eventually discover the secret of fire, now that they were aware of its existence. Although there is merit in working things out on your own, he had set out to teach them the arcane arts, and so he did. "If Zeus doesn't ignite trees with his lightning, then you could also create fire on your own. Let me tell you about flint."

**

Tartarus Bound

Prometheus awoke when he heard cracking branches from a careless person's footsteps. He looked to the sleeping humans and their extinguished fire. Earlier they had renewed the flames under his guidance. Now that they no longer needed to perpetually feed it, the humans had allowed it to go out. They rested assured in their knowledge that they could start it again, if they desired to do so.

He rose to meet the approaching people. A moment later two Olympian guards armed with swords approached the camp. "Prometheus, you are under arrest."

Around him the humans awoke from their slumber. They reacted to the hostile tone of the Olympians and waved their spears at them in a menacing way.

Prometheus smiled at the swordsmen. "As you can see, you are outnumbered."

One of the guards wrinkled his nose. "How can you stand the stench of these savages? I think I'm going to be ill."

The other guard narrowed his eyes. "Don't be a fool, Prometheus. There may only be two of us, but we are better armed and better trained than these creatures. I ask you, will you come peacefully?"

A tug on his sleeve alerted Prometheus to the presence of the human leader. "My Lord," the savage man said. "Do these men bother you? Shall we slay them in your honor?"

Prometheus patted the man's hand. "There is no need. It already honors me that you are willing to defend me. However, I am capable of looking after myself. I shall accompany them to Zeus's domain."

"But, my Lord, what will happen to you?" the leader asked. "Will we see you again?"

"I do not know," Prometheus replied. "But it does not matter. The important thing is that you know the secret of fire. Go and wield it to the benefit of all."

As the leader grunted in affirmation and withdrew, Prometheus extended his arms with his wrists held together. "I will indeed accompany you on my own accord. Lead the way."

***

At the palace Prometheus was ambushed by a red-faced Zeus. Contrary to the images that circulated, the real Zeus had a slightly disheveled look about him with his scraggly beard and wild hair. The paunch of his belly documented his taste in opulent feasts and sweet wine. Prometheus towered a solid ten inches above the Olympian god. "You!" Zeus bellowed. "You have swindled me for the last time!"

Prometheus did not even flinch at the outburst. Zeus's tantrums were well known. "Whatever do you mean, honorable Zeus?"

Tartarus Bound

The god pointed at Prometheus with a pudgy finger. "You know full well what I'm talking about. You stole my fire, and what's worse, you shared it with those filthy humans."

"Oh, I might have," Prometheus said. He shot an insolent smile at Zeus. "But I won't admit to anything. Can you prove your accusations?"

The god's features darkened, and his skin took on a shade of even deeper red. "This is the last straw, my friend."

Zeus held up his index finger. "First you trick me into leaving the best parts of the animals to humans, with the bones and scraps going to the gods, supposedly as a token of worship."

Next, the god raised his middle finger. "Then you steal fire.

"But the final insult is lying to me about it." Zeus raised his ring finger, holding up three fingers in total.

"In my defense, I—" Prometheus planned to lull Zeus in with a charming explanation of what was going on, but the god interrupted him.

"No! Be quiet and listen," Zeus said. "You've disobeyed me for the last time. I'm tired of your little schemes and dread the—"

"But mighty Zeus," Prometheus said as he started another attempt to placate the raging god.

"Be. Quiet." Zeus stared at him with madness in his eyes. He extended his arm toward Prometheus. An instant later a bolt of lightning shot toward the Titan. A deafening roar of thunder accompanied the impact.

Muscles spasming, Prometheus flew backward. He smashed against one of the white pillars. Still stunned from the bolt, he nevertheless felt that he had broken some bones. Prometheus fell to the ground, and smoke rose from the smoldering dark spot on his chest.

"Mighty Zeus," he said with a croaking voice. "I bow to your wisdom and gladly accept a term in the prison of Tartarus."

Zeus approached the fallen Titan. The god had a malicious glint in his eyes. Prometheus's ears were still ringing from the thunder, but somehow he managed to hear what Zeus told him. "As you said, I can't prove anything. Therefore I won't send you to Tartarus. Your punishment will be carried out on Earth, among those wild men that you adore so much."

Panic rose inside of Prometheus. "Mighty Zeus, you can't—"

"Oh, trust me, I can," Zeus said. He yanked Prometheus up by his hair then flung him into the arms of the palace guards. "Begone!"

***

Tartarus Bound

Stripped of his coat and power, the nude Prometheus was chained to a rock somewhere on Earth. One of the guards approached the Titan. He showed the captive Prometheus a birdcage. "Zeus isn't content with merely imprisoning you. Here's your real punishment."

Inside of the cage sat an eagle, which the guard released. The animal tried to hack off the guard's finger, but the man swiftly withdrew. Instead, the bird of prey descended on the helpless Prometheus and began to tear open the Titan's skin with its beak. Prometheus cried out as the eagle began to pick at his liver.

The guards withdrew and left Prometheus to his fate. Thanks to his supernatural healing abilities, his liver and torn skin grew back during the night. On each new morning the sadistic bird drew blood with its beak, tormenting the chained Titan. Prometheus expected to grow accustomed to the continuous assault. Instead, his rejuvenated tissue was particularly tender.

He resigned himself to being captive until the end of days, or at least until his chains had become brittle enough for him to break. After decades of waiting and being ripped apart, something unexpected happened.

His humans were no longer the savage men that Prometheus had created. A long boat appeared in the distance. Through the haze of pain, Prometheus focused on its approach. The boat moored in the distance, and a hero climbed the rocks. When the man reached Prometheus, the eagle attacked, but the hero fought off the bird. With angry screams the eagle retreated. It circled Prometheus and his rescuer for a while before eventually flying away.

"I thank you for rescuing me," Prometheus said.

The man smiled. He raised his sword that he had used to drive away the eagle. The blade crashed down on the chains, splitting them in half. "This is what heroes do. No need to thank me."

Prometheus rubbed his aching wrists. He admired the buff man with his curly hair. "Regardless, you freed me and have earned my gratitude. What is your name?"

"I'm Heracles, champion of the downtrodden."

"I am the Titan Prometheus. Zeus himself cast me out and banished me from his palace. The eagle you chased away constituted my punishment."

Heracles rubbed the beard on his chin. "I see. It is a strange world."

Since he had missed key developments on Earth and the realms beyond, Prometheus was inclined to agree. "The world is peculiar, indeed." He wondered whether there was more to Heracles's remark, however. "Is there anything in particular you're referring to?"

Tartarus Bound

"I am just thinking," Heracles said. He walked around on the rocky plateau, pointing at the Titan with his sword and then swiping the weapon in an arc at the surrounding landscape. "You are of supernatural origin. If anything, you should be imprisoned in Hades or Tartarus, yet you remain here on Earth. Several mortals, on the other hand, are spending their days in Tartarus."

"What?" Prometheus felt anger rising inside of him. "The gall of that Zeus knows no bounds. How many are there?"

"I know of at least two," Heracles said. "Tantalus and Sisyphus were mortal kings, and they were both sent off by Zeus himself."

Prometheus straightened at the prospect of interceding on behalf of his subjects. "I must free them!"

Heracles raised his left hand. "Before you do anything rash, consider this: they were both bad people—they deserve punishment."

"Of course," Prometheus said. "I can agree with that, if they are wicked men. However, mortals should answer to mortal courts. This is not a matter fit for Zeus's judgement. I have to break them out."

Heracles looked troubled. "Are you sure that you're not just doing this to spite Zeus?"

Prometheus smiled. "Perhaps there is an element of that as well. However, friend Heracles, what I said is also true. You cannot negate a true statement with another nugget of truth, so it is settled. I will go, because I cannot not go."

Heracles bowed. "Very well. Safe journey and good luck." He threw his blade into the air. It rotated around, and Heracles caught the tip of the sword on its way down. He offered the weapon to Prometheus with the handle first. "Here, take this."

Prometheus accepted the sword. He smiled in appreciation of the gesture, even though it would not do him much good in a real fight. "Thank you. Before I go, please tell me everything about Sisyphus and Tantalus and their punishment."

Prometheus listened with growing horror as the hero recounted their tales.

***

Prometheus found his sky barque in the same spot where he had left it so long ago. No mortal had dared to touch his property. He could not blame them considering the brutal punishment meted out by Zeus for any infraction against the gods.

Once he was on board he entered the interior cabin. A cool breeze blew from a grate in the ceiling to refresh him. Without care Prometheus tossed the sword into a corner. He

Tartarus Bound

retrieved undergarments and a leather coat from a wardrobe in the back of the cabin. "There, much better."

Satisfied, he moved to the front of the cabin. Opposite the window a cushioned chair was bolted to the floor. Prometheus let himself fall into the comfortable seat. His hands reached for a console that was attached to the armrest. With the push of a few buttons his sky barque retracted its anchor and rose into the air. Prometheus heard the water dripping down the hull of his barque. The acceleration pressed him into the chair as the sky barque shot straight up. Merely a few clouds obscured the sky, and the ground was nowhere to be seen in the window ahead.

Tartarus lay below Earth, below Hades even, but instead of travelling through a maelstrom Prometheus decided to travel the long way around. Since he did not expect any obstacles on this Tartarus-bound route he transferred control to his sky barque. Prometheus reclined his chair until he almost lay in a horizontal position. It would be a long journey, so he closed his eyes to catch some well-deserved rest.

***

Prometheus awoke when his barque rocked a bit on the shores of Tartarus. He blinked a few times. His bones ached—apparently even the comfortable reclining chair proved to be unpleasant after hours of sleep. Prometheus got up and cracked his stiff neck.

He left the barque and jumped into the knee-deep water. The sky of Tartarus loomed in ominous dark purple, almost black, shades above him. The water had a red hue to it, which reminded him of blood. Prometheus strode ashore. With uneasy steps on the gray gravel he approached the gate of a structure made of black rock that rose high up into the air. *This must be the prison Tartarus,* he thought.

Two guards waited by the gate. They regarded Prometheus with wary eyes. "Who goes there? What is your business?"

"I am the Titan Prometheus," he said with confidence. "I am here to take some prisoners home with me."

The guards looked at each other then back at him. "Prometheus? They say you've been imprisoned for all eternity."

"Well, it looks like *they* were wrong," Prometheus said. He glared at the two men. "Now step aside. I haven't got all day."

When the guards did not move, he lowered his voice. "For a moment I thought you defied one of the Titans. Surely that is not the case?"

Even the guards could not miss the unmentioned threat. When given the choice of facing Prometheus's wrath now or

Tartarus Bound

Thanatos's ire later, they chose the lesser of two evils. The guards stepped aside and opened the gate.

Prometheus stepped into the depths of Tartarus with a grin on his face.

As he walked the corridors he witnessed depressing scenes whenever he peeked through the bars of the cells. One time he saw the daughters of Danaus with their water buckets as they tried in vain to fill the cracked bathtub that would cleanse them of their sins. Despite the futility, they kept trying, caught in an infinite loop.

Another time poor Ixion spun around on a burning wheel. Prometheus could barely stomach the screams of the ignited man as the flames consumed his flesh. He reached for the door, but reason overpowered his compassion. If he freed Ixion now, the guards would notice from the noise alone.

Sorrowful Prometheus averted his gaze. He could not save everyone.

Still, he vowed to try again on his way back. He wandered around to get a feel for the place before formulating a plan. Had he not snatched the Olympian fire without the gods' notice? Breaking out a few mortals should be easy in comparison. While planning his route he decided that he would first release Tantalus, then Sisyphus, and finally Ixion. He debated whether he should unlock the cell of the Danaids, but his sky barque would already be cramped with four people, let alone fifty.

No, releasing the three prisoners would have to be enough for now. At Tantalus's cell an equally morbid display awaited him. Instead of seeing a king, Prometheus looked at a man that reminded him of a skeleton that was wrapped in wrinkled parchment for skin. The poor creature reached for a fruit that hung on the branches of a tree. It looked like he would reach the fruit, but then the branches moved farther up, denying him sustenance. Both the tree and Tantalus stood in a pool of water.

Eventually Tantalus gave up on the food. Instead he bowed down to cup a handful of water, but before his fingers touched it, the fluid gurgled down cracks in the ground. When all the water was gone Tantalus stood on a dry salt plain. The jagged edges of the crystals bit into his skin.

Enraged, Prometheus shoved his lock pick into the opening. He turned the key as soon as the key bits had gripped the locking mechanism. Prometheus rushed to Tantalus. He passed a flask of water to the withered man, who drained it with greedy gulps.

"Careful, not so fast," Prometheus said.

Tantalus did not heed the warning. Between coughs he said, "Thank you, thank you, thank you."

Tartarus Bound

"It's all right," Prometheus said. He smiled and picked an apple from the tree. "Here, eat something as well."

Tantalus devoured the fruit.

Prometheus put Tantalus's arm around his shoulder and dragged the weakened man toward the exit. "We must leave this place. Come quickly."

They walked through the mazelike dungeon but had to stop every once in a while to avoid patrolling guards. Prometheus's experience as a rogue and trickster came in handy.

They reached the next prison door, but before Prometheus could insert his skeleton key, Tantalus held him back. "No, not him. Let's go. Come, come."

Prometheus frowned. "What's the matter?"

Tantalus pointed at the cell. "This Sisyphus—he's a bad man."

Prometheus nodded. "I know, but so are you. I came to help you regardless."

With an unpleasant, whining voice Tantalus beseeched him. "This is different. Please, we must go."

"No, I won't have it." Prometheus shook his head. "I came here to rescue as many mortals as I can. If you don't like that, you can go back to your cell, but I won't abandon anyone."

Tantalus whimpered but did not argue the point further with Prometheus.

To his surprise the door was not locked. "What is going on?"

Prometheus and Tantalus stepped inside of the cell. A vast barren landscape littered with hills and mountains stood before them. On the peak of many mountains, round boulders rested in precarious states. The slightest touch would cause them to topple and roll down.

Prometheus's gaze wandered to a boulder that lay motionless on a plain. He needed a moment to understand what had happened. Apparently Sisyphus had rolled the boulder up the hill so many times that eventually the boulder had levelled the hill.

A voice sounded from the side. "Impressive work, isn't it?"

Prometheus and Tantalus turned around to witness the approach of a muscular man with fiery eyes. Tantalus shrank back. "Oh no, he's here. Go. We must go."

Prometheus tried to tell him with a gesture to hold his peace. He addressed the newcomer. "It is very impressive, indeed. I heard that Sisyphus is condemned to repeat a mindless, strenuous task that can never be completed."

Sisyphus laughed at that. "Initially that was the intention. Zeus and Thanatos were always jealous of my

Tartarus Bound

cunning, but I usually got the better of them. Did you know that I imprisoned the latter during their first attempt to lock me up?"

"Yes, yes," Prometheus said. "That is well known and got you into even more trouble in the end. But what is this?" He pointed at the many boulders.

"Oh, this?" Sisyphus laughed again and wiped a tear of joy from his eyes. "When faced with an impossible, repetitive task, I simply asked myself if there was any way to complete it. Zeus and Thanatos counted on me pushing the boulder up a mountain and then despairing as it rolled off the peak. For a while they got their satisfaction as I repeated the same activity over and over again, but then I balanced the initial boulder at the top. Granted, it's not stable, but that wasn't one of the provisions. I completed the task and was free to go."

Prometheus looked at the human and his unnerving, eerie, and smug grin. "Then why didn't you leave?"

Another mad laugh escaped the man's lips. "Trade in this? For nothing in the world! Only through constant practice, constant repetition, could I achieve such mastery. I'm happy where I am, and …" For the first time he seemed to notice Tantalus. "Wait a moment. Why are you here? Get back to your cell!"

Tantalus backed away, but before he could go anywhere Sisyphus jumped him and put him into a headlock. "I will personally take you back!"

"Leave him alone," Prometheus said.

Sisyphus's head snapped toward Prometheus with the look of a crazy person on his face. "He's a criminal and must serve his term. Maybe you are a criminal, too. Who are you?"

Prometheus straightened. "I am the Titan Prometheus!"

Sisyphus's eyes narrowed. "You mean you're the traitor Prometheus. As far as I know you were chained to a rock on Earth."

"I used to be, but as you can see I'm here now," Prometheus said. He nodded toward the grappled Tantalus. "Release him."

Sisyphus shoved Tantalus to the ground. He dusted off his hands. "All right, Titan, I let him go. However, both of you are still not leaving this place."

Prometheus snorted. "Who's going to stop us? You?"

There was an evil glint in Sisyphus's eyes. Before Prometheus could defend himself, Sisyphus spun around and dropped him with a kick to the head.

The stunned Prometheus dropped to the ground. He saw that Tantalus attacked Sisyphus, but a casual punch dropped the weakened man again. As Prometheus tried to get up a

Tartarus Bound

shadow fell over him. He looked up to see Sisyphus's face with that sadistic smile. Sisyphus's fist connected with Prometheus's nose, and the world sank into blackness.

***

When he awoke, someone was dragging Prometheus across the floor by his leg. Prometheus groaned as sharp stones bit into his unprotected skin: he did not wear his coat anymore. His blurry vision focused on Sisyphus, who marched on, heedless of Prometheus's discomfort. "Where is Tantalus?"

"Oh, you're awake," Sisyphus said without even turning around. "I locked him up in his cell. There's no cell for you, but I devised something else."

At their destination Sisyphus pressed the struggling Prometheus against the face of a rock. Sisyphus twisted Prometheus's arms until they were above the Titan's head. Iron manacles snapped onto Prometheus's wrists. Truly he was Tartarus-bound, but not in the way he had imagined.

"You Titans and the Olympians are so alike. You're always meddling in mortal affairs. We don't need to be rescued, and we certainly don't care for being patronized. Mankind is doing fine even without a divine benefactor."

Prometheus coughed. "What's going to happen to me?"

Sisyphus regarded him with cold eyes. "You're going to serve your term. Ah, there is your warden."

Prometheus heard the flapping of wings before he saw the new arrival. His heart sank when he realized that the eagle had returned to torment him for all eternity.

The End

About the Authors

A. H. Archer

A. H. Archer has published the award winning science fiction short story "Evakuierungsbefehl" under a different pen name.

Elisa Bonnin

Elisa Bonnin is a doctoral student of oceanography at the University of Washington in Seattle. She grew up in the Philippines and was always very fascinated by the rich mythology and interesting mythical creatures there, which was the inspiration for the story A Midsummer Night.

Tirzah Duncan

Tirzah Duncan writes novels, short stories, and poetry. She enjoys martial combat, and loves the pen and sword in nearly equal measure.

You'll also catch her bounding around Europe and geeking out about its history, obsessing over her favorite fandoms, role-play storytelling, talking aloud to herself, and trying her hand at theology and philosophy.

She thinks she'd make an excellent companion to rebel time lords and consulting detectives, and is still largely convinced that Narnia is just a wardrobe away. She wants to be C.S. Lewis when she grows up.

Katharina Gerlach

Katharina Gerlach is an author from Germany. Her homepage can be found at http://www.katharinagerlach.com/

Kai Herbertz

Dr. Kai Herbertz was born in Düsseldorf, Germany in 1977. He is a scientist by profession, as well as an indie author and indie game designer.

In August 2015 he published his medieval fantasy novel called "Age of Torridan" via Kindle Direct Publishing.

His opinions can be found in his blog at https://kaiherbertz.com/

Matthew Hughes

Matthew Hughes is a well published author with 18 novels published by large and small presses and sixty-odd sales to pro magazines. Full details can be found at www.matthewhughes.org

A.M. Kremer

A. M. Kremer is a history enthusiast and author who spends a huge amount of time researching the Middle Ages, a time period that is also the setting for most of her novels. Apart from historical fiction, she also writes the occasional fantasy story. When not writing, she can often be found travelling to various reenactments or practicing Historical European Martial Arts.

Michelle Proulx

Michelle Proulx is a Canadian speculative fiction writer. She loves everything sci-fi and fantasy, and can usually be found wandering around with a cup of tea in one hand, a book in the other, and a laptop wedged precariously under her arm. Find out more about her and her writing (including the award-winning *Imminent Danger And How to Fly Straight into It* YA Sci-Fi novel) at www.michelleproulx.com.

Juliana Rew

Juliana Rew is a software engineer and former science and technical writer for the National Center for Atmospheric Research in Boulder, Colorado. She has recent stories in The Colored Lens, Mad Scientist Journal, and Perihelion SF. Her Y/A SF novellas, "Erenarch Academy" and "Miranda of Daris," have been published by World Castle. Her author website is julianarew.com.

Danielle E. Shipley

Danielle E. Shipley is the author of the *Wilderhark Tales* novellas, the novel *Inspired*, and several other expressions of wishful thinking. She has spent most of her life in the Chicago area and increasing amounts of time in Germany. She hopes to ultimately retire to a private immortal forest. But first, there are stories to make.

Ariana Tiens

Ariana Tiens has previously written several short stories that she has presented at book readings.

Edd Vick

Edd Vick is a graduate of the Clarion SF Writing Workshop. His stories have appeared in magazines including Asimovs, Baen's Universe, and Analog, and anthologies including First Contact Cafe, Fundamentally Challenged, and Northwest Passages. His story "Moon Does Run" from Electric Velocipede was chosen for inclusion in Year's Best SF 12. By day a bookseller, he lives in Seattle with SF novelist Amy Thomson and their adopted daughter Katie (also five chickens, a cat, and a dog).

Made in the USA
Charleston, SC
16 February 2017